"Let me show you to your room. You need to rest."

And even though she knew she shouldn't, she leaned into his touch and said, "Will you be here when I wake up?"

His thumb caressed her cheek so tenderly that she had to close her eyes. When was the last time someone had touched her like they cared? Nothing about her presence here benefited Oliver, directly or indirectly. She was nothing but a risk. And yet he was still being kind to her.

She needed to move. She needed to do something, anything. But all she seemed capable of was standing there and letting Oliver stroke her cheek. She was so tired.

She almost exhaled in relief when his hand fell away, breaking that connection. But then he set down her suitcase, and the next thing she knew, she was cradled in his arms. "I've got you," he said as he carried her up the stairs. "It's all right. I've got you."

All she could do was rest her head against his shoulder. It wasn't all right. It might never be okay ever again.

But right now he had her.

And that was good enough.

* * *

His Best Friend's Sister is part of the First Family of Rodeo trilogy from Sarah M. Anderson!

Dear Reader,

Welcome to the All-Stars rodeo, an all-around circuit owned by the Lawrence family. Three siblings run the rodeo—but not everyone loves it.

Oliver Lawrence actually hates the rodeo. He's too busy to deal with it anyway, seeing as he's CEO of Lawrence Energies. So when his best friend's sister, Renee Preston, suddenly appears in his office, he's more concerned with his schedule than with the irritating little girl.

Except Renee isn't a little girl anymore. She's a widow who's four months pregnant. But if that weren't bad enough, she discovered her family's financial firm has pulled the largest pyramid scheme ever and it's all come crumbling down on her. She needs a place to hide.

Oliver doesn't have time to add another item to his to-do list, but Renee isn't a thing and she's not the same little girl he remembers. She's a woman, and there's something about her that makes Oliver forget all about the family business, the rodeo and his to-do list. When Renee's scandal catches up to them, will Oliver choose her or his family?

His Best Friend's Sister is a sensual story about fighting for your dreams and falling in love. I hope you enjoy reading this book as much as I enjoyed writing it! Be sure to stop by sarahmanderson.com and sign up for my newsletter at eepurl.com/nv39b to join me as I say, "Long live cowboys!"

Sarah

SARAH M. ANDERSON

HIS BEST FRIEND'S SISTER

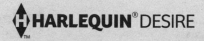

Recycling programs
for this product may
not exist in your area.

ISBN-13: 978-1-335-97146-3

His Best Friend's Sister

Printed in U.S.A.

Sarah M. Anderson may live east of the Mississippi River, but her heart lies out West on the Great Plains. Sarah's book *A Man of Privilege* won an *RT Book Reviews* Reviewers' Choice Best Book Award in 2012. *The Nanny Plan* was a 2016 RITA® Award winner for Contemporary Romance: Short.

Sarah spends her days having conversations with imaginary cowboys and billionaires. Find out more about Sarah's heroes at sarahmanderson.com and sign up for the new-release newsletter at eepurl.com/nv39b.

Books by Sarah M. Anderson

Harlequin Desire

The Beaumont Heirs

Not the Boss's Baby
Tempted by a Cowboy
A Beaumont Christmas
His Son, Her Secret
Falling for Her Fake Fiancé
His Illegitimate Heir
Rich Rancher for Christmas

First Family of Rodeo

His Best Friend's Sister

Visit her Author Profile page at Harlequin.com, or sarahmanderson.com, for more titles.

To the ladies of the YMCA water aerobics classes. Twice a week, you all listen to me babble about plot points and encourage me to keep moving, even on days when I hurt. Thanks for all your support and for laughing at my silly stories!

One

"I thought you hated the rodeo."

That voice—Oliver Lawrence knew that sweet voice. Except it was richer, deeper. It sparked memories—memories of smiling, laughing. Of having fun. When was the last time he'd had fun?

He couldn't remember.

"But here you are, surrounded by pictures of the rodeo," she went on. He could hear the smile as she spoke. She'd always smiled at him. Even when he hadn't deserved it.

Oliver jerked his head up from where it had been buried in his hands. It wasn't possible. *She* wasn't possible.

But there Renee Preston stood, just inside the door to his office as she studied the framed pictures of the

All-Stars that Bailey had artfully arranged along one wall of the office.

Although her back was to him, he was stunned to realize that he recognized her anyway. The pale gold of her hair fell halfway down her back in artful waves, the curve of her backside outlined by a dark blue dress.

How long had it been? Years? He shouldn't even recognize her, much less have this visceral reaction to her. Seeing her now was a punch to the gut, one that left him dazed and breathless. And all he could think was, *I hope she's real.* Which made no sense. None at all. But given the headaches he'd had running Lawrence Energies—why were Mondays so awful?—he wouldn't be surprised if his sanity had taken a breather.

He stared but she didn't move. Bad sign. "Renee?" He blinked and then blinked again when she didn't turn around.

Okay, he was having a bad morning. Because the truth was he did hate the rodeo—the Lawrence Oil All-Around All-Stars Pro Rodeo. He'd hated it ever since his father had won the circuit in a poker game thirteen years ago. But there weren't many people who knew it. It was bad for business if the CEO of Lawrence Energies, parent company of Lawrence Oil—and, by default, the All-Stars—publicly announced how much he hated his products.

So how did Renee know?

His assistant, Bailey, came charging into the room, looking flustered. Finally Renee moved, tilting her head to look at him. "Mr. Lawrence—I'm sorry," Bailey said, breathing hard. He gave Renee an accusing look. "She's *quick.*"

Thank God Oliver wasn't hallucinating the arrival of the last person he'd expected to see today. Renee Preston was actually in his office in Dallas in the middle of a Monday morning.

"It's all—"

But just then, Renee turned the rest of the way around and Oliver got a look at her in profile. Her little button nose, her sweetheart chin, her gently rounded stomach that curved out from the rest of her body...

Wait.

Was she *pregnant*?

Slowly, Oliver stood. "Renee, what's going on?"

Bailey hung his head. "Should I call security?"

Oliver waved away. "No, it's fine. Ms. Preston and I are old friends." That was not exactly the truth. Her brother, Clinton, was an old friend. Renee had always been an obnoxious little sister who, when she teamed up with Oliver's sister, Chloe, had been a real pain in the butt.

The full impact of her appearance hit him. She gave him a soft little smile that barely moved a muscle on her face. He didn't like that smile. It felt unnatural somehow.

He looked at her dress again. Maybe it wasn't dark blue. Maybe it was black. She looked like she'd decided to stop by his office—some fifteen hundred miles away from New York City—on her way to a funeral.

"No calls," Oliver said to Bailey. If Renee Preston was here, wearing a funereal dress while pregnant, something had gone wrong.

Suddenly, he remembered the email from Clint Preston. Had it been two months ago? Or three? Ever since Oliver's father, Milt, had uprooted the family from their Park Avenue address in New York City and relocated them to Dallas, Oliver and Clint hadn't exactly kept up a friendship. But he remembered now—that odd email that had been sent at four in the morning. *Look after Renee, will you?*

Oliver had never replied. He'd meant to, but…honestly, he'd been confused. Why did *he* have to look after Renee? She had a family. She was a grown woman. It hadn't seemed urgent, not at this time.

Clearly, it was urgent now.

Just when he thought things couldn't get any worse, they did. Served him right for thinking that in the first place.

"Actually," she said after Bailey had closed the door after him, "it's Renee Preston-Willoughby now."

Instead of pulling his hair out, he attempted to smile at Renee. "Congratulations. I hadn't heard." Although…hadn't Chloe said something about Renee getting hitched? It'd been a few years ago and Oliver had been in the middle of what was basically a corporate takeover of the business from his father.

That particular piece of information did nothing to shine a light on why she was in his office. He hadn't seen her since...

Five years ago at her brother's wedding? And Renee had still been in college. He remembered being curious because she hadn't been the same little girl in pigtails.

In fact, she'd been gorgeous, her smile lighting up the room even in the hot-pink bridesmaid's gown. But she'd had a boyfriend and Oliver wasn't going to poach another man's girl, so he'd appreciated the way she had grown into a lovely young woman from the safety of the bar, where he'd been getting sloshed with a bunch of Wall Street financiers who wanted to know if *everything* really was bigger in Texas.

Oliver dimly recalled his growing frustration that no one had believed him when he'd said he'd give anything to be back in New York City. To those idiots, Texas had sounded like a vacation. Barbecue, babes and bulls—as if that was all anyone did in Texas. All the cowgirls in the world hadn't made up for being stuck running the family businesses—and the family—then and it didn't make up for it now.

Besides, cowgirls tended to go for Flash, his younger brother. Not serious Oliver.

He almost hadn't come back to Dallas after that wedding. He'd woken up with a killer hangover and a new resolve to tell his father where he could shove the All-Around All-Stars Rodeo and his ten-gallon Stetsons and his stupid fake Texan accent. Oliver was going back to New York, where he belonged.

But he hadn't. He couldn't go back on his word to his mother. So he'd done the next-best thing—wrestled control of Lawrence Industries away from his father. The old man was still chairman of the board, but Oliver was CEO of the whole thing. Including the damned rodeo.

His attempts to relocate corporate headquarters to New York after the takeover had failed, though. Some days, he thought he'd never get out of this godforsaken state.

Had he and Renee spoken at the reception? Had she asked about his rodeo? Had he been drunk enough to tell the truth? Damn.

Even in that sad sack of a black dress, she was still the most stunning woman he'd ever seen. He wanted to sink his hands into her silky hair and pull her against his body and *feel* for himself that she was really here. Even her skin seemed to glow.

But as he looked closer, he saw other things, too. Beneath her tastefully understated makeup, he could see dark shadows under her eyes. Was she not sleeping? And even as she stood there, submitting to his inspection, her left hand beat out a steady rhythm on her leg, a *tap-tap-tap* of anxiety.

He was staring, he realized. He had no idea how long he had been staring at her. Seconds? Minutes? When had Bailey left?

He cleared his throat. "Well. This is unexpected. What brings you to Dallas?"

Her stiff little smile got stiffer. "Actually," she said, taking a deep breath, "I'm looking for Chloe." Her voice cracked on Chloe's name and she turned around quickly, but not quickly enough. Oliver just caught the way her face crumbled.

He took a step forward before he knew what he was doing. He had the oddest urge to put his arms around her shoulders, to take some of the weight from her. But he didn't. It wasn't like she'd come for him. And he couldn't imagine that she'd welcome what was essentially a stranger giving her a hug. So instead he pulled up short and said, "It's rodeo season."

She was silent for a moment, but she nodded. "And Chloe is the Princess of the Rodeo," she said in a wistful way.

Renee had been the tagalong little sister and then the bridesmaid. He knew nothing of her life. But she was clearly in distress and that bothered him.

His job was to solve problems. He'd promised his mother, Trixie, on her deathbed that he would keep the family from falling apart. That's why he was the CEO of Lawrence Energies instead of taking another job—one that didn't involve managing his father and his siblings. That was why he was still in Texas instead of going back to New York City. That's why he sucked it up and managed the damned rodeo.

Renee Preston-Willoughby was a problem and he had no idea how to solve her.

"She's in Lincoln, Nebraska, right now—and after that, it's Omaha. And after that…" He shrugged, although Renee couldn't see it. "It's rodeo season," he finished lamely. "I think she'll be back in Fort Worth in a month."

Chloe opened and closed every show in the All-Stars circuit. She had for years. She lived out of a suitcase for months on end, all because she liked to dress up in a sequined cowgirl top and ride her horse into the arena, carrying the American flag.

Oliver didn't know how his sister could stand it. He *hated* the rodeo. The swagger of the cowboys, the smell of the horses and cattle, the idiocy of people who voluntarily climbed on the back of wild horses and angry bulls—yeah, that included Flash. There was nothing he liked or even tolerated about the All-Stars.

Now more than ever—what with Chloe demanding that she should be given a chance to prove she could run the thing and his father digging in his heels and insisting that only Oliver could do it. Never mind that Oliver absolutely didn't want to do it or that Chloe would do a better job because she actually *liked* the damned rodeo.

"I should've guessed," Renee said, her voice a little shaky. He saw her shoulders rise and fall with a deep breath and then she turned around, her face curiously blank. "I'm sorry I barged in on you," she said, her voice placating. He liked that even less than the fake smile. "Thank you for not calling security on me. It's been good seeing you, Oliver."

This day just got weirder and weirder. She had her hand on the doorknob before he realized that she was waltzing out of his office just as quickly as she had waltzed in.

He moved, reaching the door just as it swung open. He slammed it shut with his hand, causing Renee to squeak. "Wait," he said and then winced as his voice came out in a growl.

He was too close to her. He could feel the warmth of her body radiating through her clothes, through his. He should step back, put some distance between them. She was pregnant, for God's sake. Who knew what else was going on?

Slowly, she turned. Close enough to kiss, he dimly realized as he stared down into her soft blue eyes. She gasped, her eyes darkening as she looked up at him through thick lashes. He was powerless to move away. "Renee," he said, and his voice came out deeper than normal. "Why are you here?"

He wasn't sure what he expected her to do. He wasn't all that surprised when her eyes got a wet look to them—it went with the dress. But then her mouth opened and instead of a sob, a giggle came out. "You don't know," she said, her eyes watering even as she laughed harder. "Oh, God—you really don't know?"

So he was out of the loop on the New York scene. "Know what?" A tear trickled down her cheek and he lifted his other hand to wipe it away. When it was gone, he didn't pull his hand away. He cupped her cheek and kept stroking her skin. It was almost like a hug, right? "What's happened?"

"Oh, nothing," she said, an edge of bitterness creeping into her voice. "It's just…" The giggle ended in a hiccup that sounded suspiciously like a sob. "It was all a lie, wasn't it? My entire life has been a lie."

He caught another tear before it could get far. "I don't understand."

"Don't you? I can't believe you haven't heard." She closed her eyes and he could feel the tension in her body. "They're calling it the Preston Pyramid. My family's investment company was nothing but a pyramid scheme and it's all come crashing down."

How could he *not* know? The collapse of Preston Investment Strategies wasn't just a New York scandal. Renee's father—with the help of her brother and her lying, cheating husband—had bilked hundreds of thousands of investors out of millions of dollars all across the country. She'd thought everyone knew about the Preston Pyramid.

But then again, wasn't that why she was in Dallas instead of New York? She just needed to get away. Away from the reporters camped out in front of her apartment building. Away from the gossip and the threats. She needed to go somewhere where people might not look at her like she was the Antichrist's daughter. And Clint had told her to trust the Lawrence family. He'd said Oliver would take care of her, but Renee was done with people telling her what to do.

Chloe had been her best friend, once upon a time. Chloe never took crap from anyone. Chloe would help her.

Except Chloe wasn't here. Oliver was. And Renee was out of options.

This was how far she'd fallen. Slipping past his executive assistant, barging into his office and doing her level best to keep it together.

Which was hard to do when he was touching her so tenderly. Not that those tender, sweet touches would last when he realized the true magnitude of what had happened. She stared at him as he processed the news. She saw her own emotions reflected in his face. Shock, disbelief—a lot of disbelief. "Your father ran a pyramid scheme? How?"

She shrugged. She should move away from him. He basically had her pinned against the door and was staring down into her face with his intense brown eyes. But he kept stroking her cheek and she couldn't break the contact. It took everything she had not to lean into the touch, not to ask for more.

It had been Clint's wedding, hadn't it? The last time she'd seen Oliver Lawrence? She remembered Crissy Hagan, another one of the bridesmaids that Renee had thought was a friend until about six weeks ago. Crissy had gushed about how gorgeous Clint's old friend was, but…Renee had blown Crissy off. Oliver wasn't hot—

he was irritating. He'd always looked down upon her. He'd been serious and grumpy, even as a kid. He'd never liked her and he'd made it difficult for anyone else to like him. Why he and Clint had got along, she'd never known.

When Renee had found herself next to him at the bar, she'd tried to strike up a conversation by asking about the rodeo. He'd promptly informed her he hated the damned thing in the meanest voice she'd ever heard.

Oliver Lawrence was not someone she could rely on. At least, he hadn't been.

She still didn't know if he was or not.

But Crissy had been right. Oliver had been hot then—and he was hotter now. He was one of those men who was just going to get better looking with age. How old was he? Twenty-eight? Twenty-nine? Clint had turned twenty-nine in jail, so Oliver was around there.

He was not the same boy she remembered. He had four inches on her and he seemed so much...*more* than she remembered from five years ago. Taller, broader. More intense.

Stupid hormones. She was not here to lust after Oliver Lawrence, of all people. She was here to hide.

"Apparently," she said, remembering he had asked a question, "very well. No one caught on for years. Decades. He generated just enough returns that people believed the lies he sold them. Reinvestment, they called it. He convinced everyone to reinvest the profits they made, sometimes investing even more than the original amount. Of course there were no real profits," she said, her emotions rising again. She struggled to keep them in check. "There were never any profits. Not for the investors. It all went to him." She swallowed, forcing herself to look away from Oliver's intensity. "To us. I didn't know anything about it, but there's no denying that I benefited from his schemes. I can't *believe* you haven't heard," she repeated.

Anger and shame burned through her. She was so damned mad at her family—and she hurt for all the people who'd been swindled. Her father had ruined lives so he could buy a fourth vacation home. It was evil, what he'd done.

But worse than that—how could she have gone twenty-six years without realizing that her father was nothing but a glorified con artist?

When Oliver didn't say anything, she glanced back up at him. His jaw was hard and there was something dangerous in his eyes. "Okay," he said. "Your father bilked investors out of a lot of money. I'm going to guess that your brother had something to do with it?"

"Of course." She sighed. "Clint and my husband were both involved."

Abruptly, Oliver stepped back. "I'm sorry I missed your wedding. How long have you been married?"

"I'm not anymore." She took another deep breath and squared her shoulders. She wouldn't let this fact hurt her. She wouldn't let Chet hurt her, not ever again. "Chet Willoughby is dead."

Oliver recoiled another step as if she'd slapped him and then turned and began to pace. "I understand that it is unforgettably rude to ask, but are you..." He waved toward her midsection.

She almost smiled. After the last two months, his apologetic question was the least rude thing she'd heard. "Four and a half months."

Oh, the press had had a field day with that. Preston Pyramid Princess Pregnant! had blared from every newspaper and website for days. *Weeks.* The media loved a good alliterative headline.

Oliver burrowed his fingers in his hair, causing his brown hair to stand up almost on end. "Right. Your family's fortune was stolen, and your husband, who worked for your criminal father, is dead, and he left you pregnant. Am I missing anything?"

The fact that there was no judgment in his voice, no sneering or laughter—that was when Renee realized she'd made the right choice. Even if Chloe wasn't here, getting out of New York was the best thing she could have done. She could breathe in Texas. That's all she wanted. Just enough space to breathe again. "Those are the basics. Oh, my mother took what was left of the money and ran away to Paris. That might be an important detail."

It was an *extremely* important detail to the authorities.

"Yes, I can see how that might be significant." He launched a wobbly smile at her, as if he couldn't tell if he should laugh or not. When she couldn't so much as manage a chuckle, he leaned against his desk and pinched the bridge of his nose.

If she'd had any other options, she wouldn't be here. He'd looked like he was already having a terrible day and that was before she unloaded her tale of woe upon him. Her life wasn't his responsibility.

But she had no place else to go. Getting permission to come to Texas had used all of her remaining political capital.

"Did you know about the scheme?"

She shook her head. "I am fully cooperating with the investigation. The authorities know where I am and I may be summoned back to New York at any time. I am not allowed to leave the country under any circumstance." That had been the deal. She didn't have much testimony to offer because her parents had maintained that Renee's entire job was to make the family look good. Her appearance was the only thing of value about her. At the time, it had bothered her deeply. How could her own father look at her and see nothing but a pretty face? How could he ignore her and leave her to her mother?

But now? Now she was glad that her father had kept her separate from his business dealings. It was literally the only thing keeping her out of prison.

Her main value to the authorities at this point was convincing her brother to testify against their father.

And Clint was in no hurry to do that. He was holding out for a better deal.

Oliver studied her closely, his arms crossed and his hair wild. He stared for so long that she was afraid he was going to kick her out, tell her to go back to New York and deal with this mess by herself. And she couldn't. She just couldn't. If Oliver wouldn't help her, she'd…

She'd go find Chloe. Not for the first time, she wished that her so-called friends in New York hadn't turned on her. Because really, what kind of friends were they? The kind who went running to the gossip websites, eager to spill anything that would make the Preston family look worse than they already did. Not a single one had stood by her. She'd been neatly cut out of her social circle, an object of derision and scorn.

So if Oliver called security, it really wouldn't be that different. She wouldn't blame him at all. She was nothing to him, except maybe a distant childhood memory.

"You need to hide?" he asked just as she had given up hope.

"Yes," she said, her heart beginning to pound faster.

He shook his head and muttered something she didn't catch, something about Clint, maybe? Then he looked at her and said, "I'm sorry about your husband."

One should not speak ill of the dead. It was one of the last things her mother had said to Renee before she'd disappeared with three million dollars of other people's money. But Renee couldn't help the bitter laugh that escaped her. "I'm not."

He thought on that for a moment, his gaze lingering on her stomach. Her skin flushed warm under his gaze. Stupid hormones. Oliver Lawrence was not interested in her. No one in their right mind would give her a second glance.

In fact, it was definitely a mistake that she'd come. She was toxic to everyone and everything surrounding her. Here he was, a good man, and she'd all but thrown herself at his feet.

She was desperate. But she hoped the taint of Preston scandals didn't smear him.

Please don't lie to me, she found herself praying. Even if the truth were brutal—like he was going to throw her out—all she wanted from him was the truth. She couldn't handle another person looking her in the eye and telling a bald-faced lie.

"All right," he said, pushing off the desk and crossing to her. He put his hands on her shoulders, but he didn't draw her in. He just looked at her and even though it was a risk to him for her to be here, she still knew she'd made the right choice—especially when he said, "Let's get you hidden."

Two

He did not have time for this. He was skipping out on important meetings that were guaranteed to draw his father out from his hunting lodge and stick his nose back into Lawrence Energies's business—and for what?

To rescue a damsel in distress. There was no other way to describe Renee. She had one piece of luggage: a carry-on suitcase. That was it. If she was going to be here longer than a week, he was going to need to arrange for her to get some more clothes.

"Is it very far away?" she asked, sounding drained.

He was not a gambling man, but he was willing to bet that Renee was going to be here for much more than a week. "We're going to Red Oak Hill," he told her as they drove away from the Lawrence Energies corporate headquarters on McKinney Avenue and in the opposite direction of his condo on Turtle Creek. "It's my private ranch. The traffic's not too bad this time of day, so we should be there in less than an hour and a half." By Dallas standards, that was practically right next door.

"Oh," she said, slumping down in her seat.

"The way I see it," he said, trying to be pragmatic, "you have two choices. You can either rest on the drive out or you can explain in a little more detail what's going on." Because he thought he had a decent grasp on the basics. Corrupt family, financial ruin, dead husband, four and a half months pregnant.

But a lot of details were missing. He'd told Bailey on his way out to pull up what he could find on the Preston fraud case and send him the links. He'd read them when he got to the ranch. He couldn't help Renee unless he knew what the extenuating circumstances were.

She made an unladylike groaning noise that worried him. "I still can't believe you haven't caught at least some of this on the news."

Worrying about her was pointless. He was doing the best he could, given the situation. Bailey had canceled his meetings for the rest of the day and had been given instructions in case anyone came sniffing around—and that included Milt Lawrence, Oliver's father. No one was to know about Miss Preston or Mrs. Willoughby or Ms. Preston-Willoughby.

"We're acquiring a pump manufacturer, the rodeo season just kicked off and my father is out of his ever-loving mind," Oliver said, trying to keep the conversation light-hearted. "I've been busy."

Besides, none of the Lawrence Energies family fortune was invested in Preston Investment Strategies—or their damned pyramid scheme. And he would know, since he had wrestled financial control of Lawrence Energies away from his father four years ago.

"Is he really?"

Oliver shrugged. "There are days I wonder." His father was only sixty years old—by no means a doddering old man. But the midlife crisis that had been touched off by the death of Trixie Lawrence had never really resolved itself.

He could've explained all about that, but she wasn't here to listen to him complain about his family. She was here because she was in trouble.

Look after Renee, will you?

He should have replied with questions to Clint's email then. If he had, he might have answers now.

He waited. Out of the corner of his eyes, he could see her rubbing her thumbnail with her index finger, the constant circle of motion. Otherwise, she seemed calm.

Too calm.

Oliver did not consider himself the family expert on women. That honor went to Chloe, who was actually a woman—although Flash, their younger brother, gave Chloe a run for her money.

Nevertheless, he had grown up with Chloe and a healthy interest in women. He was not comfortable with the idea of Renee crying, but he was prepared for the worst.

She surprised him with a chuckle. "A lot of it is in the news."

Knowing Bailey, Oliver would have several hours of reading material waiting for him, so there was no point in making her relate something he could just as easily read—with a healthy sense of detachment, instead of listening to her shaky voice and fighting this strange urge to protect her.

"Tell me the part that's not in the news."

"The part that's not in the news," she said softly, still rubbing her thumbnail anxiously. "You know, I don't think my husband was ever faithful to me."

O…kay. "Then why did you marry him?"

"My parents said we looked good together. He worked for my father and my mother thought we'd have gorgeous babies, as if that was the only thing that mattered. He was suave and sophisticated and hot. We were featured on the *Vanity Fair* weddings page online. 'A Storybook Dream' was the name of our photo essay." She laughed, but it definitely wasn't a happy sound. "I wanted a small ceremony, but no. I had to have ten bridesmaids and the craziest party favors ever." He lifted an eyebrow at her without taking his eyes off the road. "Oh, yes. Everyone got a custom engraved pair of Waterford crystal champagne glasses, a bottle of Dom Pérignon with a custom label and a Tiffany & Co. silver ice bucket engraved

with our names and wedding date, as if people cared."
She sighed heavily.

It wasn't that the elite in Dallas couldn't be just as os-
tentatious in their displays of wealth—they could. Hell,
his condo was worth a few million alone and the ranch
was easily worth twice that. Dallas was not a two-bit
town by any stretch of the imagination.

But it was different here. As cutthroat as Dallas high
society could be, there was just more heart in Texas.

He must have been having one hell of an off day if
he was mentally defending this state. He hoped his father never found out that there were things Oliver actually liked about the Lone Star State. "It sounds a tad
over-the-top."

"Oh, it was—but it was a beautiful wedding. Just
beautiful," she murmured and he remembered what
she'd said.

It was a lie. Her husband had never loved her, never
been faithful.

"I am *such* an idiot," she said miserably, and that
bothered him. Strange how it did. He hadn't thought
of her in so long but now that she was here, he found
he needed to do something.

"Hardly. You were always smart enough to get the
drop on me and Clint, weren't you? I'm thinking of a
specific incident involving water balloons off a balcony. Remember?"

That got him a shadow of a smile. "That was Chloe's
idea—but I did have pretty good aim."

That shadow of a smile made him feel good. The world was bleak—but he could still make her feel better.

He drove his Porsche Spyder faster, whipping in and out of traffic. The best—and only—thing he could do for her was get her safely out to Red Oak Hill. There, she could have some peace and quiet and, most important, privacy. Once he had her settled, he could get back to town and try to deal with his schedule and his family.

"I don't know if this part is in the news yet or not," she went on, sounding resigned. "I'm sure people have been doing the math ever since I began to show—and I began to show very early, to the disgust of my mother. But do you know?" She paused for a second and Oliver tried to get his head around the fact that her mother was disgusted by her pregnancy. She looked stunning, showing or not.

But that was the sort of thing that he couldn't just blurt out. This was a rescue, sort of. He wasn't whisking her away for a weekend of seduction or anything. Definitely not a seduction. So instead, he just said, "What?"

"He woke me up early that morning and we…" She cleared her throat. "And afterward, he told me he loved me. I normally said it to him—he rarely said the words. Usually he just said, 'Me, too,' as if he also loved himself. But he was different that morning and he surprised me, and I didn't say it back."

This was far more than Oliver wanted to know. He kept his mouth shut like his life depended on it.

"And then he went to work, screwed his secretary,

gave her the rest of the day off and blew his brains out, coward that he was. By my count, there were at least three—possibly five—women at the funeral who could have been current or former mistresses."

"That seems like a lot." One would've been too many, but to think that man had had that many women on the side in a year and a half of marriage?

Chet Willoughby was clearly a bastard of the highest order. Or he had been anyway.

"And the thing was I didn't even know I was pregnant for another two and a half months. When I missed my period, I thought it was due to the stress. Isn't that hilarious?"

She turned to him and he glanced over to see a huge, fake smile on her face. "Not really."

Her smile froze. "Some people think it is. Some people think it's the funniest thing they've ever heard. That I'm getting exactly what I deserve. There's also a lot of speculation that I was cheating on him and drove him to his death." Her voice cracked.

His heart damn near broke for her. "Those people are heartless cowards." It was a good thing that Chet Willoughby and his suave face were already dead because otherwise, Oliver would've strangled the man himself. What kind of asshole did this to his wife?

"He knew the pyramid was going to fall and he was going to go with it. My mother tried to paint this as a noble thing. He wouldn't turn on my father. Wasn't that thoughtful of him? Not like Clint's going to, maybe.

And the baby?" She shook her head. "She said the baby would be a living reminder of Chet. As if I want to remember him or his betrayal," she finished bitterly.

She was crying, he realized. Softly, quietly—but tears were trickling down her cheeks.

He didn't want to know how everyone she'd ever trusted had betrayed her. Even Clint, who Oliver had thought was a good guy. It was physically painful to know that she was hurting and, worse, to not be able to do much of anything about it.

"I don't think your child would be a reminder of betrayal," he said, feeling his way as he went. "I'd think that the baby would be a testament to your strength, your courage. Others may have cut and run, but you stood strong, Renee. That's what's going to make you an amazing mother."

She gasped and he could tell she was staring at him with huge eyes. He kept his gaze firmly locked on the road in front of him. "Do you really think so?"

He nodded like he was certain, instead of shooting compliments like arrows and praying to hit the mark. "You're welcome to stay at Red Oak Hill as long as you want," he went on. Because, aside from a lucky compliment or two, shelter was the only thing he could offer her. "I'm usually only there on the weekends. I do have a housekeeper, but I can give her some time off if you'd rather be alone."

She nodded, surreptitiously swiping at the tears on her cheeks. "Will anyone else in your family be there?"

Oliver laughed. "Absolutely not. Red Oak Hill is mine. No one will know you're there."

"Thank you," she whispered and there was so much pain in her voice that, without thinking, he reached over and wrapped his hand around hers. She clung to him fiercely. "You won't even know I'm there, I promise."

Somehow, as his fingers tangled with hers, Oliver doubted that.

It would be impossible to be around Renee and not be aware of her every movement.

As soon as he got her settled, he was driving right back to Dallas. He didn't have time to comfort Renee Preston-Willoughby.

No matter how much he might want to.

Three

Renee had not expected this. Red Oak Hill wasn't a long, low-slung ranch house in the middle of dusty cow pastures. In fact, she didn't see any cows anywhere as Oliver pulled up in front of what was undeniably a grand mansion at the top of a small hill. Towering trees she assumed were red oaks cast long shadows against the sweltering Texas sun.

The house looked like something out of a magazine. And she knew quite a bit about that. Something white caught her attention on the small lake on the other side of the driveway. "Are those…swans?"

"Fred and Wilma? Yes. They came with the house."

Renee had had a terrible day. Well, given the last five months of her life, that wasn't saying much. But somehow, the idea that Oliver had inherited a pair of swans made her giggle. "Did you name them after the Flintstones or did they come with those names?"

He quirked an eyebrow at her. "Don't know if you can really name swans, per se. They don't come when called. But…" He shrugged again, a mischievous glimmer in his eyes. "They seemed like Fred and Wilma to me. They have cygnets this year. Pebbles and Bamm-Bamm."

She didn't remember Oliver having a sense of humor. Had he always been this funny? She remembered him being uptight and grumpy. A stick-in-the-mud, she and Chloe had decided once. That was Oliver Lawrence.

But was he, really? She thought back now to the water balloon fight he'd mentioned. She and Chloe had got the drop on them from the balcony—that'd been Chloe's idea. But Oliver and Clint had retaliated with a garden hose. And Oliver had been aiming the hose.

"Renee? You all right?"

She blinked and realized that he was standing at the passenger door of his sporty red convertible, hand out and waiting for her.

His lips curved into a small smile when she realized she was staring at him. Oh, heavens—she was probably making a fool of herself. Then again, that was nothing new. "I don't know." It was the most honest thing she'd said in so long…but somehow, she knew she didn't have to put on a brave face for him.

"Here." Taking both of her hands in his, he helped her from the low-slung car. But instead of letting go of her or stepping back, he stayed where he was. Close enough to touch. "I got an email from your brother a couple of months ago," he said, staring down into her eyes. "All it said was to look after you. Renee, I'm sorry I didn't follow up. If I had realized…"

She didn't know whether to laugh or cry. Oliver Lawrence was *apologizing*. To her! She didn't need his apologies, but all the same, she felt something in her chest loosen. Everyone else had abandoned her. But this man—an old acquaintance, a childhood friend at best— was sorry that he hadn't got to her sooner.

Or was this one of those things people said to smooth over the unpleasant truths? Was he saying this because he meant it or because it was a cover?

God, she hoped it was real. She blinked hard and wondered at this strange urge to throw her arms around his neck and lean into his touch. Would he hug her back? Would he wrap his arms around her and press her against his chest? Would the heat of his body reach her through her clothes and the ironclad armor she hid behind?

Or would he stand there stiffly for a moment and then disentangle himself as politely as possible to protect her feelings? She didn't know.

Just then, one of the swans—Wilma, she decided— made a weird whooping noise that broke the moment. "Let me show you around," he said, releasing her hands and getting her luggage out of the car.

She turned to look back at the mansion. There was

no other word for it. Three and a half stories of warm red brick welcomed her to Red Oak Hill. On this side, a huge wraparound porch of pristine white wood faced the lake. Trellises of yellow roses ran up the side of the wraparound porch, their sweet fragrance filling the air with every breeze.

The Preston real estate, like everything of value the family had owned, now belonged to the feds. She supposed, once all the trials were over and the sentences had been handed down, the properties and jewels and art would all be sold at auction and the money returned to the investors her family had scammed. It wouldn't be enough, but she certainly didn't have a spare billion or so lying around.

She hadn't even kept her wedding ring. They'd offered to let her hold on to the three-carat diamond in a princess setting—for now anyway—but Renee had been happy to hand it over. It had never stood for love and honor. All it'd been was another lie. Hopefully, however much they could get for that ring would help make things right.

The entrance hall of the mansion gleamed with warm polished wood—red, of course. The sweeping staircase led up to the second floor. The doorway on the right led to what appeared to be Oliver's office, with a massive desk in the center of the room and rich brown leather sofas arranged around the Persian rug.

He gave her a brief tour and started up the stairs but then he stopped and waited for her. "Doing all right?"

In that moment, Renee wished she hadn't come. Yes,

Oliver was being a perfect gentleman—and a surprisingly compassionate friend. Yes, this mansion by a pond with a pair of swans was the perfect place to hide.

But she couldn't shake the feeling that she'd put Oliver at risk by coming here. She'd done nothing wrong, but her name was ruined and everything she did—everything she touched—was tainted by the sins of her family and her husband.

She didn't want to do anything that might hurt Oliver or Chloe. She didn't want to hurt anyone anymore.

"Renee?" He came back down the stairs and stood before her. When he lifted his hand and cupped her cheek, she knew she should pull away. It wasn't right to let him care for her.

It wasn't right to care for him.

"I'm sorry," she said. Sorry for all of it.

"It's been a long day," he said, misunderstanding. And, fool that she was, she wasn't strong enough to correct him. "Let me show you to your room. You need to rest."

And even though she knew she shouldn't, she leaned into his touch and asked, "Will you be here when I wake up?"

His thumb caressed her cheek so tenderly that she had to close her eyes. When was the last time someone had touched her like they cared? Chet Willoughby had not been capable of tenderness unless it benefited him directly. Nothing about her presence here benefited

Oliver, directly or indirectly. She was nothing but a risk. And yet he was still being kind to her.

She almost exhaled in relief when his hand fell away, breaking that connection. But then he set down her suitcase and the next thing she knew, she was cradled in his arms. "I've got you," he said as he carried her up the stairs. "It's all right. I've got you."

All she could do was rest her head against his shoulder. It wasn't all right. It might never be okay ever again.

But right now, he had her.

And that was good enough.

Somehow, Oliver got Renee's heels off her feet and her legs swung up onto the bed without thinking about her bare skin against his palms too much. He couldn't get her under the covers, so he laid her on the bed, where she promptly curled on her side and shut her eyes.

Blankets. He hurried into the next room and grabbed the coverlet off the bed. By the time he made it back, she was breathing deeply and her face had relaxed.

He tucked the blanket around her shoulders, pausing only when she sighed in her sleep. But she didn't stir.

He could feel his phone vibrating in his pocket—he left the sound off because the chimes interrupted his thinking. Bailey was undoubtedly forwarding him news articles. Oliver should get some work done. He'd need to smooth ruffled feathers from canceling his meetings this afternoon.

Especially the one with Herb Ritter. Ritter had been

in business with Lawrence Energies for close to thirty years. He was mean and crotchety and, unfortunately, a damned good oilman. And he'd been Milt Lawrence's best friend ever since the Lawrence family had relocated to Texas, which only made things worse. It was bad enough he had to manage his father, but also dealing with Ritter felt like a punishment. And the hell of it was Oliver had no idea what he'd done to deserve it.

He'd kept his promise to his mother. He ran the family business and kept his father from going completely off the deep end and Chloe as much in the loop as he could and Flash—well, no one could tell Flash a damned thing. Oliver managed the damned rodeo instead of doing something for himself. Even if he wasn't sure what that *something* might be anymore.

He did his job and kept his word. Wasn't that enough? Would it ever be enough?

But even this urgency wasn't enough to pull Oliver away from Renee's bedside.

God, she was beautiful. Tired and worried and pregnant, but beautiful all the same. He wished he could go back to Clint's wedding all those years ago. If only he'd struck up a conversation. If he had reconnected with her then, maybe he would've been able to spare her some of this heartbreak.

He brushed a strand of hair away from her forehead.

His phone vibrated again. Crap. He leaned forward and brushed the lightest of kisses against her cheek before he forced himself to walk away.

He had eighteen emails waiting for him by the time he got rid of his tie, grabbed a beer and sat down at his desk. The cold, heartless truth was that he did not have the time to take care of Renee Preston-Willoughby. He was running a major oil company, overseeing expansions into solar, wind and hydropower—expansions that he had fought his father for and finally won. And the damned All-Stars had just kicked off.

Business that required his full attention.

Will you be here when I wake up?

That heartfelt plea was the only reason why he was sitting in his office at the ranch instead of heading right back to his office in downtown Dallas.

She had asked.

This was only until she was settled in, he reasoned. She hadn't even seen the kitchen yet. He wasn't comfortable leaving her, not until he was sure she would be all right. He couldn't abandon her.

So he would stay.

Two hours later, Oliver had a much better grasp on the Renee situation.

It was a hell of a mess. Preston Investment Strategies was accused of bilking investors out of over forty-five billion dollars over the course of twenty years. Renee's father, Darin Preston, had been in jail for the last two months, unable to make bail since his wife had run off with the remaining money. Clinton Preston was also in jail, although it appeared that negotiations for his testimony and a lighter sentence were ongoing. Chet Willoughby, Preston's son-in-law, had committed suicide four and a half months ago. It didn't appear that the public had made the connection between that suicide and the pyramid scheme until Clint and his father had been arrested, along with most of the other people who worked at Preston Investment Strategies.

Bailey was thorough in his research. In addition to articles from the *Wall Street Journal*, *Business Insider* and *CNNMoney*, he also forwarded articles from the *New York Post* and even the *Daily News*. Those articles were filled with sly quotes from friends and acquaintances, all taking swipes at Renee and her mother. It only got worse after Renee's mother disappeared. It seemed there was an open debate as to whether or not Renee knew that her family was corrupt or if she'd been too dim to figure it out. Either way, the pieces were not flattering. Neither were the pictures posted with them. Awful paparazzi shots, catching her with red eyes, making her look far more pregnant and jiggly than she was in real life.

Disgusted, he stopped reading the articles because they were only pissing him off. How the hell had this happened? How had Darin Preston managed to get away with this pyramid scheme for this long? How had Clint—a guy Oliver knew was a good guy—allowed himself to be sucked down to these levels? It didn't make sense. None of it did.

His phone buzzed insistently. He picked it up—hell. His father was calling.

"Yeah, Dad?" Oliver said, closing the windows on all of the information Bailey had sent him.

"You done pissed off Herb Ritter, boy," his father drawled in a thick Texas accent. "I thought you knew better than to do that."

Oliver rolled his eyes. His father had been born and raised in New York City, although his family did come from Texas. Oliver's grandfather Mitchell had abandoned Texas when Lawrence Oil Industries—the forerunner to Lawrence Energies—had made him a multimillionaire.

Milt had lived in New York full-time until he was in his forties. Before thirteen years ago, he spent no more than a few weeks in the fall in Texas every year. The Lawrence family had maintained a house here for tax purposes and because this was where Lawrence Energies was based—but his father was *not* a Texan.

He sure liked to pretend he was, though. "I've made my apologies to Ritter," Oliver said, keeping his voice level. "We've already rescheduled the meeting."

"That's not going to be good enough."

Oliver gritted his teeth and decided to change the subject before this call devolved into a shouting match. "Dad, have you heard about Darin Preston?"

Milt was silent for a moment. "That con man? I never did trust his get-rich-quick schemes." He paused, making a low humming noise in the back of his throat. He always did that when he was thinking. "Wasn't he in the news recently?"

"He was." Oliver didn't want to tell Milt that Renee was asleep upstairs. He had promised her privacy, after all.

It was the only thing he could promise her.

"Why do you ask?"

Oliver decided to hedge the truth. "I had a strange message from Clint. It seemed he was helping his father scam people."

"Now, that's too danged bad," Milt said. "Clint was good people. And his sister—what was her name?"

"Renee."

"Yeah, Renee. She and Chloe got along real well. Trixie…" He paused and cleared his throat. Oliver knew that his father's eyes were watering, not that he would ever admit to it. Even after all these years, the mention of his beloved wife choked Milt up. "She thought the sun rose and set on Renee. She used to take the girls shopping. Always made sure to include that girl whenever she could. Hell, she always included Clint when she could. But she had a soft spot for Renee." He hummed again. "Your mother, God rest her soul, didn't think too highly of Rebecca and Darin Preston. And you know she was an excellent judge of character."

Oliver considered this. He honestly had no memories of his mother doting on Renee. But then again, it did seem like the little girl had always been underfoot, hanging out with Chloe and plotting how next to irritate Oliver and Clint.

The Preston kids had eaten a lot of meals at the Lawrence table—and Oliver didn't remember going over to Clint's house very much. Hardly at all, actually. There'd been a few times he and Clint had sneaked into Clint's house to get some trading cards or the latest video games…but they always sneaked right back out and hightailed it to Oliver's house.

It hadn't struck him as odd then. But what if it'd been more than that? Clint had told him they had to be quiet—no, not quiet, but *silent*. He hadn't wanted his mother to know they were in the house. No noise and no touching anything.

Looking back now, Oliver had to wonder—had Clint been afraid of his mother?

"I read that Mrs. Preston ran off to Europe with the rest of the money."

"Hell. What a family, eh? The Preston kids were good kids, but there's only so much a kid can do when they're raised in a pit of vipers. It's a shame that they got caught up in this. At least you had your mother and me. For a while anyway." He cleared his throat again.

It was a damned shame. "I did. We all did." Most days, dealing with his Tex-ified father left Oliver frustrated and bitter. But it was true. Before Trixie Lawrence's death, Oliver had loved his parents. Both of them. For fifteen years, the Lawrence family had been happy and healthy and stable. Not everyone had that.

He'd promised his mother that he'd take care of his family. They may not be as happy or as stable—thank God they were all healthy—but at least they hadn't all been arrested and indicted. That had to count for something.

But it wasn't enough for his father. It never was. When Milt spoke again, Oliver could hear the forced cheer.

"Have you finished negotiations with ESPN about running the All-Stars?"

"I had to reschedule that meeting today. Something came up." And unlike Herb Ritter, Oliver was in no hurry to get back to this one. "You should let Chloe take the meeting. She'd do a great job."

"She's the Princess of the Rodeo and she's doing that clothing line," Milt reminded him, as if Oliver could ever forget. "I don't want that Pete Wellington anywhere near her."

Oliver rolled his eyes. He didn't like Pete Wellington any more than his father did but the man was too much a born-and-bred cowboy to ever lay a hand on a woman. As evidenced by the fact that he hadn't killed any members of the Lawrence family yet. And he'd had plenty of opportunity. "He wouldn't hurt her."

Not for the first time, Oliver considered signing a minority stake in the rodeo back over to the Wellington family. It'd been their damn rodeo before Pete's father, Davy, had lost it in that poker game. Pete had never forgiven either his father or Milt. Which meant he bore one hell of a grudge against anyone with the Lawrence last name. Oliver would be more than happy to cede a little control of the All-Stars back to Pete. Hell, if Oliver thought it would help, he'd just outright hire Pete to run the damn thing.

The only problem was Pete's pride wouldn't settle for merely working for the All-Stars. He maintained Milt Lawrence had stolen the All-Stars and he wanted it back. All or nothing.

Which meant he got nothing. Funny how winning here felt a lot like losing. "Chloe would be great in the meeting." She'd have the marketing team eating out of her hand and they both knew it.

As usual, though, Milt ignored Oliver. "She's already doing her part. You make sure you do yours." With the final *hmph*, Milt hung up.

The rodeo was good for the business, Oliver repeated silently, just like he did every single time he had to deal with the damn thing. The All-Around All-Stars Rodeo was 60 percent of their marketing and had been consistently in the black for the last six years.

That didn't mean Oliver had to like it.

He pushed the All-Stars out of his mind and focused on the problem at hand. He didn't have to like anything about the Renee situation. He wasn't enjoying this trip down memory lane, where he couldn't remember if his mother had taken Renee under her wing or not. Hell, for that matter, he still hadn't recalled how Renee knew he hated the rodeo.

He *hated* not knowing. Starting from a place of ignorance—about his childhood memories of the Preston kids, about the Preston Pyramid scam, about the woman currently upstairs in bed—that was how bad decisions got made. No matter how the saying went, ignorance was not bliss. It was disaster. And he was tired of this day feeling like a runaway train about to crash into the station.

He couldn't get off this train and continue to let it barrel down on Renee like everyone else had. Her brother and father? They hadn't so much abandoned her as they'd been taken into federal custody. But her husband, her mother—hell, even her friends—all had. No one had stood by her.

He couldn't add himself to that long, long list. Not when he thought back to the way he'd coaxed a small smile out of her when he'd told her the names of his swans. Not when she'd looked at him, trying so hard to be strong, and asked if he'd still be here when she woke up.

Not when his own father remembered Renee as a little girl who'd needed a friend.

Something had to give. He hit the number for Chloe. "What?" she said, sounding breathless.

"And good afternoon to you, too. Listen," Oliver said, bracing himself for the lie. He was not naturally good at deception. "You get to deal with ESPN. The contract negotiations are yours."

There was a pause on the other end of the line. "Is

this a joke? Because it's not funny, Oliver," she snapped. "You know Dad would never let me do anything beyond carry the flag."

"No joke," he assured her. "Consider it a…" His mind scrambled for a reasonable explanation that wasn't simply *I don't have time for this.* "A test run. You do a good job on this, and we'll give you more responsibilities. Because I think the rodeo should be yours." That, at least, wasn't a lie.

"And Dad agreed to this?" she asked, doubt heavy in her voice.

That was the problem with Chloe. She was too perceptive for her own good. "He wants the deal done." He hedged. "He wants to see how you handle this and the clothing line."

It'd been Chloe's idea to capitalize on her popularity as the Princess of the Rodeo by launching an eponymous clothing line. She'd been overseeing the development of jeans, tailored T-shirts and sequined tops with the intent of launching with this year's rodeo season. So far, so good.

But could she keep up that success and handle high-level negotiations? God, Oliver hoped so.

She was quiet and Oliver wondered if she'd say no. If she did, Oliver was screwed. "You're sure this isn't a joke?"

He was surprised at how young she sounded. "Chloe, you know I don't have a sense of humor."

"Ha. Ha. Fine." She blew out a long breath. "I can do this, you know."

"I know. I'll forward you the information and let the ESPN people know you're handling the account from here on out. And Chloe?"

"Yeah?"

He almost told her Renee was upstairs and maybe Chloe could come home for girlfriend time so he could get back to work? But at the last second, Renee's face floated before him again, a single tear tracing down her cheek. He remembered the way her skin had felt under his hands as he'd wiped that tear away.

Renee needed him. Chloe needed to prove herself with the rodeo. And maybe it was wrong or selfish, but Oliver would rather help Renee than negotiate a TV distribution deal. Besides, all he needed to do for Renee was get her settled and see what he could do to help her out. How hard could that be?

He'd keep Renee's presence here a secret just a little bit longer. He told Chloe, "Keep an eye out for Pete Wellington. Dad's concerned he's going to pull something."

"Oh, wonderful. There's nothing I love more than unspecified threats from disgruntled cowboys." Oliver heard something in her tone beyond annoyance. But before he could figure out what that was, Chloe went on, "Fine. Anything else?"

"And keep Flash out of trouble," he added, because that was what he always asked her to do. Not that it ever worked. No one could keep that man on the straight and narrow.

"You're up to something," she said, but he could hear the smile in her voice. "And when I find out what it is, you're gonna pay." With that parting shot, she hung up.

He looked at the clock on the wall. It was already three thirty. He had no idea how long Renee was going to rest but there was no shot in hell of him making it back to the office during the workday at this point.

She needs a friend. Oddly, the little voice that whispered this in his mind wasn't his own or even Chloe's—it was his mother's.

Renee was not family. She wasn't grandfathered under the long-ago deathbed promise Oliver had made. He didn't *have* to take care of her.

And yet…

She needs a friend.

Had Trixie Lawrence said that once upon a time, perhaps when Oliver had complained about how much Renee and Chloe were bugging him and Clint?

He didn't know. But one thing was clear. If he didn't do his level best to help Renee out of this situation, his mother would be disappointed in him. Or she would've been anyway.

He stared at nothing in particular and then made up his mind. If he was going to get to the truth of the matter, he had to go straight to the source. He hit his lawyer's number. "Miles? It's Oliver. I need—"

"No, no—let me guess. Did you finally strangle your

father? Or your brother? I've got twenty bucks riding on the answer," Miles Hall replied with a laugh.

"Neither." Oliver shouldn't be doing this, shouldn't be doing any of this. Funny how that wasn't stopping him. "I need to talk to Clinton Preston. He's in jail in New York City on fraud charges for—"

"The Preston Pyramid guy?"

He scowled. Did everyone know about the scam but him? Sheesh. He'd have to have Bailey add "major scandals involving people I used to know" to his morning news briefs. "Yeah. Well, the son anyway. I need to talk to him on the phone. Can you make it happen?"

Miles was quiet for a moment. "Give me thirty."

"Thanks."

Clint had a hell of a lot to answer for. Starting with why he'd helped his father steal that much money and ending with why he'd asked Oliver to look after Renee.

Then, once Oliver had his answers and made sure Renee was comfortable and safe, he could get back to work.

But the thought of making Renee comfortable, of carrying her back to bed and this time, staying with her…

Hell. He definitely had to get back to Dallas tonight.

Four

Renee came awake slowly. It was so quiet here. New York was never quiet. There was always someone shouting, horns honking, sirens blaring. A person could barely think in New York City.

She couldn't remember the last time she'd slept so deeply. Usually, it was because terrible nightmares woke her up every few hours, panting and crying. Right now, she felt surprisingly calm. She wouldn't go so far as to say peaceful, but she was thrilled with calm.

A *thunk* from somewhere below her finally got her eyes open. She started when she focused her eyes on the clock. Was it four thirty already? She had been asleep for hours. She needed to get up and…do something. What, she had no idea.

But it wasn't like her to laze the day away. Even back when she'd been little more than a trophy wife, she'd still kept busy. She'd been on the boards of several charities, including her favorite, One Child, One World. She liked helping kids but…since the Preston Pyramid collapsed, she'd resigned from all those boards rather than taint their good works with her family's scandals.

Which left her at loose ends. But it was fine. No one was missing her in New York, that was for sure. This was part of her plan to hide in Texas. If she wanted to nap, she would nap, by God.

She tossed back a blanket and forced herself from bed. It was tempting to go right back to sleep, but…

Oliver had said he would wait for her to wake up.

She was hungry and she had to pee. She stretched, trying to get the kinks out of her shoulders. Over a dresser there was a large mirror and she recoiled in horror when she caught sight of her reflection. Her hair was lopsided and her makeup had not survived the nap. Plus, her dress was wrinkled horribly, and besides, it really wasn't very comfortable.

But her lawyer had recommended that, if she went out in public, she maintain a somber, mourning appearance. It wouldn't do anyone any favors if she were seen looking frivolous or, God forbid, *happy*. Not that there was a lot of risk of that, but Renee understood the point.

Her entire life had been about keeping up appearances. The bereft widow, the horrified daughter—they were all just another role to slip into.

She tore the dress off and kicked it under the bed. She couldn't wear it for another moment, couldn't maintain the fiction that she mourned her husband.

She looked around the room. Had she fainted? She didn't remember coming into this room. She only remembered...Oliver's arms around her, holding her close. His deep voice rumbling in her ear, although she couldn't remember the words. A light touch on her forehead, then her cheek. The smell of his cologne.

She remembered feeling safe and cared for. That was all she needed.

But this was a nice room. There was a small sitting area with a low coffee table—her bag was on it. The love seat ran along one wall and a fancy desk that looked like it belonged in the parlor instead of a guest room was on the other side. The walls were a pale green and the bedding was pristine white. It was calm and peaceful and reminded her of a garden in the early-morning sun.

She took a deep breath and let it out slowly. She could breathe here.

She dug into her bag. Along with her wedding ring, she had left most of her couture and designer clothing for the feds. Her wardrobe had been worth hundreds of thousands of dollars—but it had been just another prop in her never-ending role as the adoring wife, the picture-perfect daughter. She was tired of living that lie.

She dug out leggings and a slouchy tunic. This was her normal outfit for yoga classes—but it was forgiving enough that she could still wear it comfortably. She might even get several more months out of the top. She'd love to take her bra off because the damned thing barely fitted anymore and sleeping in it had not been a good idea. But the thin, creamy cotton of her shirt wouldn't hide anything from anyone. Especially Oliver.

A chill raced over her and her nipples tightened, which was exactly why she had to keep the bra on. She really hoped Oliver wasn't involved with someone else. But the moment that thought crossed her mind, she scowled at herself in the mirror. Okay, he was amazingly hot. And yes, he was being really sweet to her. That didn't mean there was any mutual attraction here and even if there was, what was she going to do? Seduce him? Please. She was the hottest of hot messes and almost five months pregnant.

Fine. It was settled. No seduction. At least…not on her end anyway.

Purposefully *not* thinking of what Oliver might do if she paraded around braless, she used the en suite bathroom and fixed her hair and face, opting for a simple ponytail and just enough under-eye concealer to hide the worst of the dark circles. When she was done, she took stock again.

She looked not-quite-so-pregnant in her loungewear and the nap had helped a lot. She didn't look like the woman she'd been six months ago. The salon-perfect hair was gone, as was the expertly contoured foundation. And she could see the pregnancy weight rounding out her face and her arms. Her mother had called her fat right before she'd run to Paris.

No, Renee was not the same woman she'd been six months ago. Was that such a bad thing? She'd been a mannequin then. Someone to be seen and coveted but not heard. The problem was, she wasn't quite sure who she was now.

She wouldn't allow her voice to be silenced again. As she stroked her stomach, she made a promise to herself and her child—she would do better. Better than her mother. Better than Renee herself had been. She'd be... someone like Oliver's mother. Renee would be the fun mom who made cookies with her child and friends or took them for ice cream in the park. Whether she had a boy who liked fashion or a girl who played soccer, it didn't matter. Just so long as Renee was a better mom. A better woman.

She dabbed at her eyes. Stupid hormones. If there was one thing she'd learned growing up, it was how to keep her emotions on lockdown to avoid getting into trouble. But suddenly she was pregnant and hiding and she couldn't keep her stupid eyes from watering stupidly. Gah.

Besides, there was no need to get teary now. She had a long way to go before tea parties and sports. She had to start being this new, improved woman before the baby got here and it wasn't likely to happen in the bathroom. She needed something to eat and... Well, food first. Plans second.

Quietly, she made her way downstairs, listening hard for the sounds of people. A low hum seemed to be coming out of Oliver's study. He was talking to someone, she realized—probably on the phone. A wave of relief swept over her. He'd made a promise to her and he'd kept it—even if it was an inconsequential promise to hang around for a few hours. He'd still kept it.

Guilt wasn't far behind. She'd pulled him away from a workday. He was probably trying to get caught up. She shouldn't interrupt him. He'd said the kitchen was in the back of the house, right? She should go.

But then, in a voice that was more of a shout than a whisper, Oliver clearly said, "You are, without a doubt, the most vile, abhorrent, morally bankrupt *idiot* I have ever had the misfortune to know and that's saying something. You know that, right? I mean, what the hell were you thinking, Clint?"

Renee stumbled to a stop. Eavesdropping was not exactly on the moral up-and-up, but was he talking to her *brother*? How the hell had he pulled that off?

She moved to stand just on the other side of the door to his study. There were some pictures here, so she pretended to look at them. But really, her entire attention was focused on one half of the phone conversation happening in the next room.

"Yeah, she's here. What the hell, man? You send me a one-line email with no other explanation, no other context—no, I didn't know your entire family had crashed and burned. I'm busy!" This time, he was shouting. "I have my own family to manage, my own business to run—a business that does not steal money from investors! So you'll excuse me if I haven't kept up with all the ways you've destroyed your life!"

A wave of nausea roiled her stomach and she didn't think it was morning sickness.

"No, I know." He said this in a weary voice, and Renee honestly couldn't tell if it was better or worse than him shouting. "Yeah, she told me. How could you let her marry someone like that?"

Renee bristled. Her brother was not her keeper. She was a grown woman capable of making her own decisions and her own mistakes, thank you very much.

That, however, hadn't stopped her from wondering the exact same thing a hundred times over the last few months. Clint had known who Chet was. They'd both worked for her father for several years before the wedding. And yet her own brother had done nothing to warn her that she was marrying a serial cheater and a con artist.

It was hard not to be bitter when there was so much to be bitter about. Growing up, she and Clint had stuck together. So much of her childhood had been the kids against the parents. Even when they'd fought—and they *had* fought—they'd still protected each other from the icy punishment of their mother and the casual neglect of their father.

But when she'd really needed her brother, he hadn't been there for her.

Instead, it was Oliver who was mad on her behalf. Oliver who was defending her.

"That's a shitty excuse and you know it," Oliver snapped. "She trusted you. Your investors trusted you. Hell, I trusted you. And you did nothing to earn it…No, I'm not going to take it out on her. I'm not a monster, unlike some people I know…Yes," he said, sounding defeated. "She did? I thought you two were going to go the distance. But I guess she couldn't live being married to a snake oil salesman." Another pause. "Renee really didn't know, did she?…I didn't think so. Look, I said I'd take care of her and I meant it. Enjoy your time in jail, buddy."

Renee sagged against the door frame as relief pushed back against the nausea. Oliver believed she hadn't been a part of the scheme. He understood, at least on some level, how badly the betrayal by her family had hurt her.

She shouldn't have come here. She shouldn't have listened to the phone call, either. She didn't want to put Oliver at risk for being a decent human being to an old friend and she didn't want to put either of them in a position where he felt like he had to lie to her.

But she was so glad she was here.

"Renee? Will you come in here?"

She jumped, her heart racing. Had he known she was listening the entire time? Oh, heavens. *Busted.*

She swallowed and felt her face go pleasantly blank, felt her shoulders square up and her chin lift. The reactions were hard-wired at this point and she was helpless to stop them.

With one final deep breath for courage, she stepped into the study.

And stumbled to a stop.

Oliver was leaning against his desk, his ankles crossed and his arms folded in front of his chest. He looked very much like he had earlier—had it only been this morning?

But the differences. Oh, the differences! He'd lost his suit jacket and his tie. His white button-up shirt was now open at the neck and he had cuffed the sleeves, revealing strong forearms. And strangely enough, he was barefoot.

Oh, dear God. He'd made business professional look good but he was making casual look positively sinful. Her mouth went dry and for a moment, she forgot how to speak.

Then everything got worse and better at the same time because he notched an eyebrow at her at the same time the corner of his mouth curved up into a smile, revealing a dimple she didn't remember being there before. Had she ever really seen him smile like that? He was so impossibly gorgeous that her mouth disconnected from her brain, and she blurted out, "I wasn't listening," like an idiot because obviously she had been.

That got his other eyebrow in on the action. But instead of calling her on her juvenile defense, his gaze swept over her. Her skin flushed as he took in her shirt, her leggings, her own bare feet. When he lifted his eyes, Renee could tell that, even from across the room, they were darker, more intense.

Was it hot in here or was it just her?

"I see the nap did wonders for you," he said, his voice low and serious and nothing like how he had sounded on the phone with Clint.

It was broiling in here. She was starting to sweat. "I hope you don't mind that I changed into something more comfortable. Since I have no plans on going back out into public today. Or tomorrow," she finished lamely.

"Or even the day after that?" he teased, pushing off the desk and coming to stand in front of her.

Renee knew not to show fear. Showing guilt was even worse. She had trained herself to keep her head up and her eyes open, no matter what cutting comments or terrifying punishments her mother had decreed.

But this was Oliver. Serious, grumpy, stick-in-the-mud Oliver. And he was smiling down at her, warmth and humor in his face and maybe just a little concern as he said, "My house is yours for as long as you need it. I want you to be comfortable here. I want you to be yourself," as he settled his hands on her shoulders.

Wonderful. Her eyes were watering *and* she was sweating. Maybe she should've stayed in bed a little longer. "Do you know—" and she was horrified to hear her voice waver "—that no one has ever wanted me to just be myself?"

His smile faded. But then his thumbs began to rub little circles on her shoulders and she didn't know if she was getting closer to him or if he was getting closer to her. Maybe they were both moving, drawn together by strange circumstances and an even stranger attraction.

Whatever it was, she found herself in his arms, her breasts pressed against his chest, her chin tucked in the crook of his neck—and her bare toes brushing his. The contact felt shockingly intimate, and for a moment, she forgot how to breathe.

It wasn't right, how much she sank into his touch. It certainly wasn't proper, the way she wrapped her arms around his waist and held on as if her life depended on it.

"I'm sorry I eavesdropped," she muttered against the collar of his shirt. "And I'm sorry I lied about it. I'm… still getting used to honesty." It didn't sound any less lame, but at least it was the truth.

"It's all right," he said softly, and one hand began to rub her lower back in small, delicious circles of relief that made her sigh.

"How did you know I was listening?" She'd thought she'd been quiet. But not quite enough, apparently.

"I heard you get up. I'm sorry you heard me call your brother a vile idiot."

"Even if he deserved it?"

Oliver chuckled, a rich sound that rumbled out of his chest. "Especially if he deserved it." He leaned back and Renee looked up at him. This close, she could see the flecks of gold in his brown eyes like hidden treasure.

Something in her chest tightened as he stroked the finger over her cheek and down her chin. "Renee..."

She held her breath. God, she needed...something. She needed to hear the truth.

But then again, what was the truth here? She was naive and gullible at best? Complicit? An idiot, vile or otherwise?

She'd work on facing the truth soon. Tomorrow. Right now, she desperately changed the subject. "Thank you for being here when I woke up."

"I gave you my word. I keep my promises."

She shouldn't, but she couldn't help herself. She buried her face against his shoulder and automatically, his arms tightened around her. "That's...that's good to know," she mumbled against the collar of his shirt. "Not everyone does that."

"I'm not everyone."

Thank God. But she didn't say it out loud. Instead, she said, "Now what?"

"Hmm." She could hear the steady thrum of his heartbeat. That was what made him safe.

But what made him dangerous was the way his body began to rock almost imperceptibly, pulling her along into a rhythm. What made her weak was the way his hand splayed out against the small of her back, pushing her into his solid chest.

Her nipples went painfully hard and given how very little separated him from her, she was sure he could feel those hard points against his chest. Her cheeks flushed and she shivered at unbidden images of her in Oliver's arms, but with far less clothing and far more moving.

Oliver was everything and nothing she needed right now. She absolutely was not thinking about sex, especially not with him. She still hadn't determined if he was involved with anyone else, for crying out loud! She wasn't interested and she wasn't looking to get lucky. End of story.

Good lord, it was hot in here.

And he still hadn't answered her question. That *hmm* didn't count, especially not when she was breathing in the scent of his cologne—something light and spicy and warm that smelled perfect on him.

Then, so slowly she almost missed it, he began to pull away. His arms loosened around her chest and he leaned back to look down at her again. But even then, he kept letting go of her, one moment at a time. "I need to get back tonight," he said, his voice low and serious and perfectly Oliver. She didn't know if that was supposed to be a good thing or not. Was he happy he was getting out of here before she lost her composure again? Or was she only imagining that there was a hint of regret in his tone?

"That's…" She cleared her throat and broke the contact between them. "That's fine. I'm sure you have someone waiting on you to get home." She had to turn away when she said it.

It was for the best if he left. She'd come here for the

peace and quiet, right? And she definitely didn't feel peaceful when Oliver was around. Far from it.

He snorted. "Renee."

She put her face back together. She could do this. She didn't want to worry him and besides, she was probably just hungry. And pregnant. It wasn't a great combination. "Yes?"

He'd retreated back to his desk. She could feel the distance between them and, irrational as it was, she hated it. "I won't leave until you're settled."

She bit back the laugh. She might never be settled again. But instead, she said, "I appreciate it."

"I won't be able to get back out here for a few days," he went on, sounding nothing like the man who'd been holding her moments ago. "But if you need anything— clothes, medicines, weird foods—just let me know. I'll plan on spending at least part of the weekend out here."

Was he coming to see her or to babysit her? "All right."

He looked at something on his computer and then put his phone in his pocket. "And to answer your other question," he said, walking back toward her, "no, there's no one waiting on me at home. But I do have to work tomorrow. It's…"

"Rodeo season," she finished, trying hard not to smile. It shouldn't matter that he was available and that she was—well, maybe not available. But certainly un-attached.

But it did.

"Dinner?" he said, a friendly smile on his face. His dimple didn't show.

Right. He was being friendly because they were friends and nothing more.

"Dinner," she agreed.

At the very least, it was good to have a friend.

Even if he was Oliver Lawrence.

The whole drive back to Dallas, Oliver tried to solve the problem that was Renee Preston-Willoughby.

He failed.

Instead of running through viable solutions to keep Renee safe and secure for the short and medium term— possibly up to and including the birth of her child—he was thinking of how she'd looked when she'd stepped into his study this afternoon. Gone were the hideous black dress, the dark hose and the understated black pumps. And in their place...

Oliver did not know a great deal about women's fashion, but he recognized the kind of clothes Renee had been wearing. Chloe loved to knock around in the same kind of leggings and loose tops.

It was safe to say that he had a vastly different reaction to Renee in leggings than he did his sister.

The top had come to just below her hips, leaving every curve of her legs outlined in tight black fabric. It'd taken everything in his power not to picture those legs wrapped around his waist at the time. The last thing anyone needed was for him to get a raging hard-on at the exact moment she'd needed to be comforted by a platonic friend.

Now? He adjusted his pants. He had a long drive ahead of him.

Damn, this was ridiculous. He had a million things he needed to do and none of them involved replaying the way Renee's body had fitted against his over in his mind. What he should be doing was talking to Bailey and getting caught up on everything Oliver had missed while he was out of the office today. Yeah, his executive assistant had probably already left work for the day, but Oliver was the CEO and if he needed Bailey to work late, then Bailey worked late.

Then again, Bailey was always talking about his wife and the latest adorable thing their two-year-old son was doing and Oliver would feel bad interrupting his dinner. A man should spend time with his family. He should be involved in the lives of his children.

No, Oliver couldn't in good conscience bother Bailey after work hours.

Which apparently meant he was going to think about Renee. She had looked so much better after her nap. Still tired, still worried—but she'd been softer. Not as brittle.

That made him feel good. He had given her that.

But that was all he could give her. It didn't matter how much his body responded to hers, how much it hit him in the chest when she smiled—or how much it killed him when her eyes watered but instead of crying, her whole face went oddly blank. What he wanted didn't matter.

He would repeat that sentiment until he got it through his thick skull.

Because it didn't matter that he had finally given in to his impulse and pulled her tight in his arms in the office. It made no difference when he'd felt the tension drain out of her body and it didn't matter that, a moment or two later, he felt the different tension begin to work its way through her. It had no bearing on anything that being around Renee was a slow burn of torture.

Oliver was no angel. He'd been caught up in the throes of lust from time to time. Those affairs had always burned white-hot but fizzled out after a matter of months, if not weeks. He and his lady friends had parted ways with a smile and a fond farewell.

So he knew this attraction wasn't just lust. His whole body was *not* on fire for Renee Preston-Willoughby.

Had he seriously told her that he wouldn't be back until maybe the weekend? That wasn't right. She was all alone in the middle of nowhere in a strange house. Yes, he'd shown her how to operate the stove and where the pantry was and walked her through the remotes for the televisions. He'd even left her with keys for his ranch truck, in case she needed to get to Mineola, the closest town.

But what if something went wrong? What if she had a medical emergency? What if someone figured out where she was—someone who did not think kindly of the Preston family?

He almost turned his Porsche around. He could stay

the night and make sure everything was okay and then get up and...

Okay, getting up at four to slink out the house wouldn't help anyone. And she was a grown woman who could navigate New York City by herself. She wasn't a child or an invalid. She'd be fine.

At least for the night.

Maybe he'd go back out tomorrow night, after work. Just to make sure she was doing all right.

Yeah. He'd do that.

That's what friends were for.

Five

She was going to bake.

Renee stood in the massive kitchen at Red Oak Hill, surveying the row of copper pots hanging from a pot rack over a massive island in the middle of the kitchen with stools tucked along one side. The countertops were a cool gray granite and the cabinets were cream with an aged patina. A Subzero fridge, better suited to a restaurant than a house with only one person living in it part-time, commanded almost half of a wall.

She didn't know how to cook. Or bake. No one in her house had cooked growing up. On the few occasions they'd suffered through dinner as a family, either Rosa, the undocumented Guatemalan maid her mother had constantly threatened with deportation, had prepared a meal for them or they'd had food delivered in. Nothing good ever happened at those family dinners. She shuddered at the memories and absently rubbed her leg.

Otherwise, her parents ate out—separately, of course. Breakfast had been cold cereal to be eaten as quickly and quietly as possible before she and Clint made their escape to school because waking her mother up before noon was a surefire way to suffer.

Instead, she had happy memories of boisterous meals with the Lawrence family where everyone bickered and told jokes and only sometimes did she and Chloe switch out sugar for salt or drop peas in Clint and Oliver's milk. If anyone yelled, they were laughing when they did it and no one ever jabbed silverware into someone else's legs.

She had afternoon teas with Chloe and Mrs. Lawrence after they'd gone shopping or seen a show or even just because. She had fun afternoons with Mrs. Lawrence teaching her and Chloe how to bake cookies and cakes. Then Renee and Chloe and sometimes even Mrs. Lawrence would eat their creations with a big glass of milk while watching cartoons. Those times were all the more special because…

Because of Mrs. Lawrence. She'd been warm. Loving. *There.* How many times had Renee dragged her feet when it was time to go home? How many times had she prayed for Mrs. Lawrence to be *her* mother, the Lawrence family *her* family? Her and Clint's. They could've been happy there. They *had* been happy there, all the happier because it was such an escape from home.

Mealwise, not much had changed when she'd married and moved into her own condo with Chet. They'd eaten out most of the time, often separately because Clint was working late or entertaining clients or dating other women, probably. And Renee hadn't seen the point in cooking just for herself, so she'd gone out with friends. Everything else had been delivered. Cooking wasn't a priority, not with some of the best restaurants in the world just a short phone call away.

Renee Preston-Willoughby didn't do anything so menial as prepare food.

That was going to change, starting now. Besides, she was dying for some cookies. Giant gooey chocolate chip cookies, just like she'd made all those years ago with Chloe and Mrs. Lawrence. With ice cream. Did Oliver have ice cream? If he were here, she'd ask him. But she wasn't going to wait around for someone else to solve her problems. Even if that problem was just ice cream related. She'd check the freezer herself.

Besides, what else was she going to do with her time? She could sit around and feel sorry for herself, but that was self-indulgent in the extreme. In addition to her nap yesterday, she'd had a solid night's sleep. She'd eaten breakfast, lunch and dinner for the first time in…a while. Last night Oliver had made these amazing burritos that he had had seemingly pulled together out of thin air and there'd been leftovers. Marinated chicken and steak and a corn salsa that was possibly the best thing Renee had eaten in months, plus tortilla chips and cheese. Lots and lots of cheese. It wasn't true cooking, but she'd assembled her own food today and that was a start. A *good* start.

It helped that, for the first time since her husband's funeral, food tasted good. Suddenly, she was starving.

She scrolled through Pinterest, looking for a recipe that promised both delicious and easy cookies.

It took a long time to assemble the ingredients. She had no luck tracking down baking soda, but baking powder was close, right? They both had *baking* in their names, after all. And it said *1 tsp* of both baking soda and salt. How much was a tsp? She found a measuring spoon that had a *T* on it. *That must be it.*

At least there were chocolate chips. Really, that was all that mattered.

She wished Oliver were here. The peace and quiet of this big mansion out on the countryside was wonderful, but she'd love to share it with him. This morning, she'd walked around the small lake, watching Fred and Wilma as they cut gracefully through the water with two baby swans trailing after them. Oliver had a small dock on the far side, so she'd kicked out of her flip-flops and sat with her toes in the water, watching the breeze ruffle the leaves of the huge red oaks.

This afternoon, she'd sat on the porch with a big glass of iced tea and, surrounded by the scent of roses, watched dusk settle over the land. She'd watched a few episodes of her favorite TV show—the animated one about a diner Chet had thought was stupid. And she'd taken another delicious nap.

No one had yelled at her. No one had accused her of horrible things. No one had mocked her appearance or told her that her husband had got exactly what he deserved. All in all, it had been a nearly perfect day.

Except she wished Oliver had been here. Which wasn't fair. He had to work, she knew that. As she dumped the sugar onto butter, she knew she didn't need Oliver by her side. But she wanted to show him that she was doing all right. Better than all right.

She'd been fragile and shell-shocked when she walked into his office, exhausted with worry and drained from the flight. But that didn't define her. It bothered her that he might think that was all there was to her.

But then again, she had a hazy memory of him telling her that she was strong for her unborn child. So maybe he knew? Or maybe he'd just been polite.

No matter. He would be here this weekend and by then, she hoped to have figured out the secret to perfect chocolate chip cookies.

The sugar blended into the butter—at least, she hoped that was what *creamed* butter and sugar was sup-posed to look like—she checked the recipe again. Dang, she'd forgotten to turn on the oven. The recipe said it was supposed to preheat—maybe she should crank it up? Would it preheat faster that way? It was worth a shot. She set the oven to five hundred and then went back to her recipe. It called for one cup of chocolate chips, but that didn't seem like enough. So she doubled it. One could never have too much chocolate.

There. She had something that reasonably looked like chocolate chip cookie dough. If she wasn't pregnant, she'd test it, just to make sure it tasted right. But raw cookie dough was one of those things that pregnant women weren't supposed to eat, so she resisted the temptation. She scooped out the dough and set the sheets in the oven.

It was ridiculous, how proud she felt of this small accomplishment. Putting cookies in the oven to bake barely counted as an accomplishment at all. But still. She'd done it. God, she hoped they were good.

"What's going on in here?"

Renee screamed in alarm as she spun, losing her balance and bouncing off the corner of the island. Seconds later, strong hands had her by the arm, pulling her against a warm, solid chest. Tingles raced down her back and she knew even before she got a look at his face that, once again, Oliver had caught her before she fell.

She shouldn't be this happy to see him. But she was anyway. "You're here!" she said, breathless as she wrapped him in a big hug. *Now* the day was perfect.

"I am," he said, as if he were just as surprised to find himself back at the ranch—and in her arms—as she was.

Oh. *Oh!* She was hugging him, feeling every inch of

his hard body against hers. She took a quick step back and let her hands fall to her sides. "I didn't think you were coming back tonight."

He leaned against the island, his mouth curving into a smile that sent another shiver down her back. "I wanted to make sure you were doing all right."

Something warm began to spread in her chest. "You could've called." After all, it wasn't like he'd popped next door to check on her. He had driven a solid hour and a half out of his way. He wasn't even in his suit. He was wearing a purple dress shirt but he had on dark jeans that sat sinfully low on his hips today. God, he looked so good. Better than chocolate chip cookies.

"I could've," he agreed.

His dimple was back and Renee had an inexplicable urge to kiss him right there on that little divot.

"Is everything all right?" If there was bad news, she could see him wanting to deliver it in person because that was the kind of man Oliver Lawrence was.

He wouldn't hide from the unpleasant truth. But instead of lowering the boom, he said, "Everything's fine."

They were words she'd heard hundreds, thousands of times. Chet had said them constantly, including in those last months when their lives had begun to unravel, even though Renee hadn't known it at the time. But she'd been able to tell that things weren't fine. But that's all Chet—or her brother or her father—had ever told her, like she was a toddler who'd bumped her head and needed a simple reassurance.

Those words coming out of Oliver's mouth were different. She was pretty sure. God, she hoped he wasn't that good of a liar. "You're sure?"

He lifted one shoulder. "I have Bailey scanning the headlines for any mention of you in the greater Texas area, but nothing's cropped up. A few New York headlines are wondering where the pregnant Preston Pyramid Princess has disappeared to, but it's more because they're sad you're not providing them with clickbait fodder. Your brother hasn't accepted a deal yet. Your soon-to-be-former sister-in-law gave an interview to the *Huffington Post* where she eviscerated Clint, as well as your husband and your father, but only mentioned you to say that she'd always thought you were sweet and she really hoped you hadn't had anything to do with the scam. She didn't think you had."

A breath Renee hadn't realized she'd been holding whooshed out of her lungs. "Really? That's…that's great. I should send Carolyn a thank-you card. That's the nicest thing anyone's said about me in months."

"I can think of a few nice things to say about you." His voice was low and sweet, like dark honey and, as he looked her over with something that seemed like desire, her body responded. "More than a few."

Sweet Jesus, she wanted to melt into him. The space between her legs got hot and sensitive and her stupid nipples went all tight again. Which was the exact moment she remembered she didn't have on a bra.

Oh, hell! She didn't have on a bra and she'd hugged him and now he was making her blush. She crossed her arms over her chest and hoped he hadn't noticed.

He lifted an eyebrow and her face got even hotter. Of course he'd noticed.

But he had the decency to refrain from pointing out the *pointedly* obvious. Instead, he looked around the kitchen. "Baking?"

She was not disappointed that he hadn't lavished her in compliments. She was relieved, dang it. "I thought I'd give chocolate chip cookies a try. But fair warning," she said, desperately trying to keep her voice light, "I haven't baked anything in years."

He began to round up the dirty dishes without protesting or anything. "And you wanted to get back to it?"

"I do." She took a deep breath, thankful to have something to talk about that didn't have anything to do with her nipples or their willingness to turn into hard points around this man. "I have these wonderful memories of your mom taking the time to bake with me and Chloe and sometimes it was awful and sometimes we actually made something good and it was always so much…fun. Do you remember?"

Because now that she thought about it, she remembered that although Clint and Oliver hadn't been baking with them, sometimes Renee and Chloe had shared the cookies or cupcakes with them. But only when they were feeling generous.

He paused in the middle of dumping the mixing bowls in the sink. "Yeah, I do."

"Good." It made her happy to know that he still had those shared moments in an otherwise-fraught childhood relationship. "I want to have fun again. I want to be the kind of mom who enjoys making cookies and won't scream if the cookies don't turn out perfect. I want to be the kind of mom my kid looks up to, who'll…" Her voice caught in her throat. "Who'll be there for her kids. And her friends' kids."

Not like her mom had been.

The bowls clattered in the sink and Oliver turned. He studied her with that smoldering intensity of his that sent flashes of heat down her back.

But he didn't say anything. "Yes?" she finally asked nervously. She kept her arms crossed.

"I know my mother loved you. She considered you another daughter."

The sense of loss that hit her was more painful than she'd expected, mostly because she hadn't been expecting it at all. "Oh," she said, her throat closing up and her eyes watering. "That's…that's sweet. I was…" She swiped at her cheeks. "I was sorry we couldn't come to her funeral." Her mother didn't look good in black and funerals were dreary. Which meant Renee hadn't got a chance to say goodbye.

Oliver nodded. "And then we moved to Texas right after that."

It had been a one-two punch and honestly, Renee wasn't sure she'd ever got over it. She'd not only lost the wonderful mother of her best friend, she'd lost the entire Lawrence family. She'd lost the feeling of home that day.

But she hadn't been a little girl anymore. When Mrs. Lawrence had died, Renee had been thirteen and better equipped to deal with her mother's insanity. She'd joined more after-school clubs, found new friends.

Nothing had ever replaced the Lawrence family.

"Hey," Oliver said, stepping forward and pulling her into his chest. "I'm sorry. I didn't mean to upset you."

"It's okay," she replied, her words muffled by his shirt. "Sorry. Hormones. It doesn't take much these days."

"No, I'd imagine not." He leaned back, stroking his hand down her cheek and lifting her face so she had no choice but to look him in the eye. "Renee…"

Her breath caught in her throat again but this time, it had nothing to do with a spontaneous overflow of powerful feelings. Instead, Oliver's one hand was tracing slow circles around the small of her back, pushing her closer to him. To his lips. His thumb dragged over her cheek, sending sparks of electricity across her skin.

"I'm so glad you came back," Renee whispered, even as she lifted herself on tiptoe, closing the distance between them.

"I'll always come back for you," he murmured against her mouth.

Dear God, please let that be the truth. She didn't want easy lies. She couldn't bear the thought of him lying to her at all. Not him. Not now.

His lips brushed over hers, the touch a request more than a demand. She inhaled deeply, catching his scent—spicy and warm, with his own earthy musk underneath and a faint hint of something burning.

Something burning?

She jolted as he asked, "What's that smell?" at the same time a loud beeping filled the air.

"The cookies!" She twisted out of his arms and raced to the oven.

By the time she got there, smoke was beginning to curl out of the oven door. "Oh, no!" She frantically looked around for the oven mitts or…something. Anything, before she set his house on fire! But she didn't know where anything was!

Oliver picked her up and physically set her to the side. Then, as cool as a cucumber, he turned off the oven and produced the missing oven mitts. In short order, he had the cookie sheet and the nearly black puddles that had once aspired to be cookies out of the oven, a fan running and windows open to clear the room, and he was…

Laughing?

He was, the wretch. He was mocking her failed attempt at baking while he pulled the battery from the smoke detector and for a moment, it felt like they were kids again, always poking each other until the other responded. She wondered if she could hit him with a water balloon—and what he might do in retaliation. Renee tried to scowl at him, but she was suddenly giggling along with him.

"Why, in the name of all that is holy," he sputtered, dumping the ruined cookies into the sink, "was the oven set to five *hundred* degrees?"

God, she was an idiot. "Oh! I forgot to preheat it so I thought I'd turn it on high to make up for it and I must have forgot to put it back down to the right temperature."

He laughed so hard that he slapped his thigh. She had to wrap her arms around her stomach to make sure she didn't accidentally wet her panties. When she thought she had herself under control, she eyed the mud puddles. They clearly had spread beyond the ability of the cookie sheet to contain them—but now that they were charred, they weren't going anywhere. "I may owe you some new cookie sheets," she said, which set off another round of giggles.

"What did you do to those poor things?" He grabbed the spoon she'd used to scoop out the dough and poked at the closest mud puddle.

And then they were off again. God, when was the last time she'd laughed?

She couldn't remember when. How sad.

But she was laughing too hard to let self-pity take

control. She sagged into Oliver's arms and he buried his head against her shoulder, which didn't do a whole lot to muffle the almost unholy noises of glee he was making. They both were making.

Eventually, the giggles subsided. But her arms were still around Oliver and his arms were around her and he'd promised he'd always come back for her and then he'd almost kissed her, and she still wasn't wearing a bra.

"It's a good thing I came out here to check on you," he murmured against the skin of her neck.

"It is," she agreed, holding her breath. Would he kiss her again? Or let her kiss him? She shifted against him, bringing her breasts flush against his chest again. "I'd feel really bad if I'd burned your house down."

"That would've been tragic." Then she felt it, the press of his lips against the sensitive skin right below her ear.

She exhaled on a shudder as his mouth moved over her jaw. Then his lips were on hers and this time, it wasn't a hesitant touch.

This time, he kissed her like he wanted her.

Even though she knew she shouldn't because *complicated* would never be a strong enough word to describe her life, she kissed him back.

Months of sorrow and anger drifted away under the power of Oliver's kiss. Because it was an amazing kiss, sweet and hot and a seduction, pure and simple. His hands circled her waist, his thumbs tracing a path along her lower ribs. All the while, his lips moving over hers, his tongue lapping at the corners of her mouth. She opened for him and his tongue swept inside, claiming her.

Branding her as his own.

Because he wanted her. Not because she was her father's daughter, but in spite of that, Oliver Lawrence wanted her.

God, it was so good to be wanted.

So Renee kissed him back. She looped her arms around his neck and lost herself in the rhythm of their mouths meeting and parting and meeting again. Her body went hot and soft and hard all at once and she wanted him with a fierceness that left her dazed.

She wanted this to be real. She needed it to be honest and true.

But the niggling doubts in the back of her mind wouldn't be quieted. Because what if it wasn't? She couldn't bear another person lying to her.

She pulled away. Slowly, but she did—and just in time, too, as Oliver's hands had begun a slow but steady climb up her ribs and toward her aching breasts. She wanted him to touch her, wanted him to soothe the tension with his touch. With his mouth.

But she wasn't going to throw herself at him. She wasn't going to do anything until she was sure.

She had no idea what that certainty would look like, however.

He let her pull back, but he didn't let her go. Instead,

he clutched her to his chest, breathing hard. She curled into him, unwilling to break the contact.

"We should…" His voice cracked and he cleared his throat. "We should do the dishes."

"Yeah."

Neither of them moved.

He stroked her hair. "I'll need to head back tonight. I have an early meeting tomorrow."

That was a good thing. Because if she knew Oliver was asleep right down the hall, she might do something stupid, like slip into his bed in the middle of the night and pick up where they'd just left off.

Funny how him leaving didn't feel like a good thing.

"You can't miss your meetings," she said, her voice wavering just a little. "Not for me."

He made a snorting noise. "I might be able to come back out tomorrow night. Just to see how you're doing. But I can't make any promises."

She smiled and hugged him tighter. "I'm going to try cookies again."

"Maybe this time, you could follow the recipe?"

"Maybe," she agreed.

They laughed and, as if by silent agreement, pulled away from each other. "Then we better wash the dishes."

She grinned. The ways she'd messed up those cookies… "And find the baking soda."

Six

He really didn't have time for yet another three hours in the car, round-trip, plus however long it took to make sure Renee was doing okay and hadn't set the oven on fire. He'd cut out of work an hour early today in an unsuccessful attempt to beat rush-hour traffic, which meant yet another meeting with Ritter had been pushed back. That wasn't going to make his father happy.

Oliver needed to be focusing on his job. His jobs—he needed to check in on Chloe and see how the negotiations with ESPN were going.

Funny how that to-do list wasn't stopping him from making the long drive out to Red Oak Hill again.

He pulled up in front of the house, grabbed the groceries out of the trunk and bounded—bounded!—up the front steps and into the house.

The first thing he noticed was the smell. Instead of burning, something that smelled suspiciously like chocolate chip cookies wafted through the house.

Oliver grinned as he hurried back to the kitchen. Hopefully, she'd followed the recipe this time. But he made up his mind—he was going to eat the damned cookies and tell her they were great, no matter what.

Well, almost no matter what. He wasn't eating charcoal.

He pulled up short when he walked into the kitchen. The place was an utter disaster. Flour coated almost every surface and the sink was overflowing with mixing bowls. Ah—she'd found the stand mixer, as well. Cookies covered every square inch of countertop that wasn't taken up with baking supplies.

Racks and racks of cookies. There had to be eight, maybe ten dozen in all. Some were noticeably darker and some were almost flat and a few looked like they hadn't spread at all.

That was a hell of a lot of cookies.

"If we eat all those cookies at once," he said, trying to find a place to set his bags, "we'll get sick."

"Oliver!" Renee popped up from where she'd been bent over the oven. "You're here!"

He grinned at her. "I am. You've been busy, I see."

She glanced around at all the cookies, her cheeks coloring prettily. "You're out of chocolate chips. Sorry about that."

For a moment, all he could do was stare at her. The longer she was at Red Oak, the better she looked. The shadows under her eyes were a distant memory now and the lines of worry at the corners and across her forehead had faded away. True, she had a smear of flour across her forehead, but that just made her look even more adorable. She was wearing yet another pair of soft leggings and a loose turquoise T-shirt that made her eyes shine. Her hair had been pulled back into a messy braid and all he wanted to do was mess it up further.

He didn't. All he did was look. Because for the first time, Renee looked like she was meant to be—a young, beautiful woman enjoying herself.

God, she took his breath away.

To hell with his restraint. The grocery bags hit the ground and the next thing he knew, she was in his arms and he was kissing her like she was the very air he needed and he'd been holding his breath for the last twenty-four hours.

"I brought more chocolate," he murmured against her mouth before he plundered it ruthlessly with his own.

He hesitated, but she didn't pull away. Instead, her body molded itself to his, her lips parting for his tongue, her fingers sinking into his hair as she tilted his head for better access.

"More chips are good," she agreed, but Oliver had already forgotten what they were talking about.

All he could remember was that this was why he had

come. To hold Renee and discover her secrets one long, leisurely kiss at a time.

"Tell me to stop," he muttered as her hands slid down from his hair, over his back and down to his butt. She squeezed and what was left of his self-control began to fray. Badly. "Tell me to stop and I will."

She pulled away, her eyes closed, and he damn near fell to his knees to beg for her. Him! Oliver Lawrence!

But if she wanted him to beg, by God he would, because at some point, his best friend's irritating little sister had become a gorgeous young woman he couldn't walk away from.

He wasn't going to walk away from her.

"Oliver." His name on her lips was soft but he didn't miss the undercurrent of need in her voice. God, he hoped it was need.

"Yeah, darling?"

She opened her eyes and the force of the desire reflected back at him threatened to unman him right then and there. "Don't stop."

This was crazy. Worse than crazy. Dangerous, even.

She couldn't let Oliver sweep her off her feet and carry her up the stairs—again.

She shouldn't let him kick open the door to his bedroom and set her down on her feet. And under no circumstances should she let him kiss her as if she were his last chance at redemption.

There would be no redemption. Not for her anyway.

It was selfish and shallow but she just wanted to feel good again. Even if it were just for an evening in Oliver's arms. Nothing permanent. She wasn't looking for another 'til-death-do-us-part. She'd done that already.

But was it so wrong to want to feel desirable? Was it bad to want a man to look at her with naked want in his eyes, to need her so badly that he kept driving halfway across Texas to see her?

Was it an awful thing to take what he was offering?

"Renee," he murmured against her lips as his hands slid underneath her loose tunic. The touch of his bare fingers to the skin at the small of her back made her groan.

How was he doing this to her? She was no innocent—she was almost five months pregnant, for heaven's sake. She'd known desire and want in her time.

But nothing had prepared her for *this*, she realized as Oliver pulled her shirt over her head and cast it aside.

"Oh, dear God in heaven," he said, his voice revenant as he stared down at her bare chest. Because she hadn't been able to bring herself to put a too-small underwire bra on again if she were going to be alone in the house all day.

She'd planned to put the blasted thing on before he got here. She'd had the best of intentions. But Oliver had shown up earlier than she'd expected and it was rapidly becoming apparent that the bra was pointless in more ways than one.

"They're not always this big," she told him. "In the

interest of full disclosure." Because no matter what, she didn't want anything that happened in this bedroom to be a lie.

Then she waited. Really, she wasn't afraid of what he might think about her new and improved breasts. Men liked big breasts, after all. Chet certainly had.

But it was the rest of her that had her worried. Her belly had started rounding out by the time she was three months pregnant and, aside from her loose tunics and leggings, nothing fitted. Not even close.

"I've put on a lot of weight." She managed to say it in a level voice, without any of the hurt bleeding into that statement. But if he were going to say something… less than perfect, she wanted to be braced for the worst. She wouldn't let it hurt.

"Hmm." The noise rumbled out of his chest as his fingers trailed over her ribs, their destination unmistakable. "It suits you."

What the heck did he mean by *that*? But before the words got off the tip of her tongue, his fingers were skimming over the sides of her breasts, circling around her nipples.

Which were, of course, tightening to hard points. Of course they were.

His thumbs swept over the tips and Renee stopped thinking about her weight, about Chet Willoughby and how perfectly average he'd been in bed. Instead, her head dropped back and she had to steady herself as the sensation of being touched—tenderly, sweetly and oh-so-hotly—overwhelmed her.

Then something warm and wet swept over her right nipple and her eyes flew open just in time to see Oliver lick it again. "Okay to suck or not?" he murmured against her flesh.

Heat flooded her body, making her shift anxiously. The pressure between her legs was so intense that she could barely think. All she could imagine was his mouth on her. "I... Gently, I think?" Was she more sensitive because she was pregnant? Or just because this was Oliver and he was seducing her like she'd never been seduced before?

She watched in fascination as he fell to his knees before her, his hands around her waist to hold her steady. Then he looked up at her and, holding her gaze with his own, he took her right nipple in his mouth.

She couldn't have held back the moan if she tried—and she did try. But it was a pointless exercise because sensations crashed over her like waves breaking over a jagged shore.

And this was Oliver being gentle. In control. Cautious. She had a sudden urge to see him beyond all reason, wild with need and crazed with desire. For her.

As his mouth drew down on her, his thumb continued to flick over her other nipple and that pressure between her legs crested and then crested again. She dug her hands into his hair and held on tight.

She didn't want to think about all the times she'd

faked this kind of reaction, nor did she want to think about all the times Chet had skipped the foreplay to get right to the sex.

So she didn't. She made a conscious effort to put those unpleasant disappointments into a box inside her mind and shut the lid tight. Chet was dead and she wasn't. She was here and she was coming back to life under Oliver's skilled touch.

"You taste like vanilla and chocolate," he murmured as he kissed the space between her breasts before moving to the other one. "God, Renee, you taste so damn good."

She sighed and gave herself over to him. It wasn't selfish if he was giving himself freely, right? He wanted her. She wanted him. They were both consenting adults. There wasn't anything wrong with any of this.

A thought in the very back of her mind tried to remind her that, if anyone put her and Oliver in bed together—or even near the bed—there would be many things wrong with this. Her toxic reputation might very well damage his own, which might affect his business and his family.

All those lovely feelings threatened to turn sour in a heartbeat and she almost pulled away from him. She couldn't risk hurting the Lawrence family and, selfish as it was, she couldn't risk tainting all those wonderful memories from her childhood with loathing and recrimination.

But that was the exact moment that Oliver relinquished her breast and began kissing down her stomach. Renee froze, torn between the need to do the right thing, the urge to hide her belly or the marks on her legs from him and the unleashed desire still crashing through her system. "Oliver…"

He kissed the top of her belly, where it rounded out. And as much as Renee detested it, she was powerless to stop her mother's voice echoing through her thoughts.

Look at you. It's disgusting, how you've already let yourself go. It's embarrassing to be seen in public with you when you're this fat and ugly.

She moved to cover herself but Oliver caught her hands in his. "Don't hide from me, Renee," he said, his mouth moving lower. "You have no idea how gorgeous you are right now, do you?"

"I'm not." Her whisper was shaky, even to her own ears.

"You *are*." He looked up at her, that intensity shining through the lust. "Let me show you how much I want you." Then, before she could stop him, he hooked his fingers into the stretchy waistband of her leggings and her panties and pulled down.

He had to work the fabric over her hips but he was making that humming noise that seemed to come straight from his chest as he bared her. She balanced herself on his shoulders as she stepped out of her clothes and then she was completely nude before him.

He stared at her in what she desperately hoped was wonder and not something less…savory. He hadn't noticed the scars yet, so she fought the urge to slap her hands over the tops of her thighs. Maybe he wouldn't notice. Chet never had, after all.

God, why was she like this? Why couldn't she let go? Why couldn't she get lost in Oliver's eyes, Oliver's touch? Why was her mother's sneering voice cutting through this moment? Why were memories of Chet lurking just behind that?

Why couldn't this be perfect? No, that wasn't the right question, she realized as she blinked back tears.

Why couldn't *she* be perfect?

Then Oliver leaned forward and pressed a kiss to her belly button, his hands stroking up and down her thighs before moving back to cup her bottom. He squeezed as his mouth moved lower and his teeth skimmed over the space just above the hair that covered her sex. Because she hadn't been able to bring herself to keep up with her waxing. Being naked on a table before a near stranger? That was a gossip disaster waiting to happen, and besides, who was going to see her like this?

Oliver.

He crouched down a little more and nudged her legs apart. She should let go of his hair, tell him to stop. At the very least, she should insist they pull the drapes and turn off the lights. Then she would be able to hide her belly and her thighs from him and she might be able to let go.

Because she needed to let go. She needed to prove those voices in her head wrong.

She needed this. She needed *him*.

"Beautiful," he whispered and he seemed so damn sincere that she had to believe he meant it, had to believe this was real. That was when his hand slid between her legs, brushing over her core with such tenderness that she wanted to cry. Stupid hormones. Then he leaned forward and pressed a kiss right there and, miracle of miracles, her mind emptied of all the hurt and criticism and pain and there was only Oliver and his mouth and his hands and *her*. He wasn't in Dallas with anyone else. He was here because he chose her.

His tongue moved over her sensitive flesh and it was the same and it was different and it was everything all at once. Because she didn't remember all these sensations crashing over her in a flood that couldn't be held back. She didn't remember making these noises without being able to control them. And she sure as hell didn't remember being so swept away by the rising tide that her legs shook and she suddenly was in danger of falling over.

"Oliver," she begged, pulling on his hair. "I can't stand."

He looked up at her, one arm locked around her legs and that was when she saw it—the raw hunger in his eyes. It took her breath away.

Then he surged to his feet, catching her in his arms. When he kissed her again, she didn't taste vanilla or chocolate, but instead she was on his tongue and he was marking her as his own.

She couldn't think. All she could do was act. So she yanked at the buttons on his shirt and jerked at the zipper of his pants because if she was naked, she wanted him naked, too.

He kicked out of his pants as she hauled his undershirt over his head and then there was nothing between them. She stepped back to see what he looked like underneath his button-up shirts and suit jackets. She got the impression of broad and lean and muscled with a smattering of chest hair. But she barely had time to say, "Oh, Oliver," before he was kissing her again, his hands pulling her hair from her braid as he backed her up.

So she let her hands explore. His chest was hard and warm and he hissed against her lips when she caught his nipples with her fingernails. His stomach rippled with muscles as she moved her hands lower and then…

"Oh, *Oliver*," she moaned against the skin of his neck as she gripped his erection. He was rock hard under her touch and she could feel his muscles shake as her hand moved up his impressive length and back down to his base.

He stilled against her, his head on her shoulder, his breath coming hard. "Woman," he growled, skimming his teeth over the delicate skin where her neck met her shoulders, "if you don't stop that right now, you'll have to wait at least five minutes before I can be inside of you."

She did that. She made him react like that. It was powerful, knowing that she could bring him to the edge, just like he'd done to her. God, it felt good to be in control of something again.

She smiled and stroked him again. "Five whole minutes?"

He groaned against her skin and then he bit her. Not too hard, but it was primal in its own way. "Maybe only three." He grabbed her hand when she squeezed. *"Renee."*

Then he picked her up. But instead of throwing her down on the bed, he spun and sat hard on a sofa. Renee blinked. She'd been so caught up in her own thoughts and in Oliver that she hadn't even realized that his room was set up similarly to hers. There was a large—and inviting—bed done up in deep blues and a sitting area with two love seats and a simple coffee table between them.

They were on the love seat that faced the big mirror over a dresser. "I need to watch you on top," he groaned. He rolled on a condom—where had that come from?— and then lifted her up so she could put her knees on either side of his legs. "I need to see you come apart, babe."

His erection brushed against her center and she shuddered. "Awfully confident, aren't you?"

She shouldn't tease him. But this was Oliver, dang it. She'd been teasing him for as long as she could remember and she had a feeling that he wouldn't dare turn a hose on her right now. It was safe to poke at him, to smile and laugh with him. He wouldn't demand to know what was so funny or, worse, who else she was thinking of.

He caught her face in his hands and touched his forehead to hers. "Renee," he said and she didn't hear any anger or insult in his voice. "I promise you, I won't leave you behind." There was a touch of sadness in his eyes as he said it.

Her throat closed up and her eyes watered. But she put on what she hoped was a sensual face. "I know."

He pressed a kiss to her lips that, considering their position, was surprisingly sweet. "Don't tell me what you think I want to hear, babe. Tell me what you need. Because I won't leave you frustrated." His hips flexed, dragging his erection over the folds of her sex and instinctively, she lifted herself up. His tip lodged firmly against her center and she gasped, her legs shaking again. "One way or another," he promised, "I'm going to make you scream with need." And there was nothing sweet about *that*.

It was hard to breath. Because he meant it. He meant every last word and in that moment, she fell in love with him. How could she not?

She lost her half-hearted battle with gravity and sank down onto him. For a long moment, they both sat still, breathing hard. Renee couldn't think, couldn't feel anything but Oliver inside of her, Oliver filling her. He was a part of her now. He always had been, but this?

"Woman," he growled again. "I can't—I need—oh, God." His fingers dug into her hips and he lifted her up before guiding her body back down again. She moaned as he filled her.

"I had no idea," he ground out, the cords on his neck standing out as he held himself in check. Then he caught her left nipple in his mouth and tugged, ever so gently, while she rose and fell and rose again. Each pull of his lips drew an answering pull from where they were joined and she was helpless to hold on to anything but him. "That's it, babe," he growled, moving to her other breast. "Take what you need."

And she fell a little bit more in love with him because he was waiting for her. And even if he came first, he'd still take care of her. He wouldn't leave her behind. She wasn't just here for his pleasure. He was here for hers, and *that*? That made all the difference in the world.

She lifted his face and kissed him with everything she had. He groaned into her and that sound of pure need was her undoing. Renee came apart in his arms, her body going tight around his as the wave crested and broke over her.

She collapsed against his chest, unable to do anything but breathe hard as he thrust up into her, his hips moving harder and faster. "Renee," he said, somewhere between a groan and a shout. "Babe!"

She clenched her inner muscles at the same time she bit him on the shoulder and he made a noise of pure animal pleasure, so raw and desperate that she came a second time as he gave her everything he had.

Legs and arms everywhere, they didn't move, except for the panting. "I had no idea," Oliver said, his voice shaking. He leaned back and looked at her. "Okay? Or do you need something more?"

How could she not love him? Because no one—not a single one of her previous boyfriends—had ever asked. And if she'd tried to ask for something else, they'd taken it as an insult to their manhoods. It was her fault if she hadn't come, not theirs.

But Oliver was a different man. A better one.

God, it'd be hard to leave him when the time came.

But that was still a ways off. Hopefully at least a few more weeks. She didn't dare look further ahead than that.

Right now, she was going to live in this moment for as long as she could.

"Better than okay," she said, kissing him again as she lifted herself free. "So much better."

Oh, she liked that grin on him. Then, because on some level, she was apparently still ten and he was still thirteen, she added, "But we might need to try that again later, just to be sure this time wasn't a fluke."

His eyes popped open in surprise and she tried not to laugh, she really did—but that was a battle she lost. A second after she started giggling, he narrowed his eyes to slits and he would have looked dangerous if he hadn't been smiling. "Why, you little tease. You know what I'm going to do?" He caught her in his arms and she wondered if maybe he hadn't been exaggerating when he'd said five minutes—maybe even just three—earlier.

"What?" She barely got the words out because he took her breath away.

"I'm going to…" He cocked his head to the side. "Do you hear something?"

"What?" That wasn't romantic. Or seductive. That didn't even count as basic flirting.

But then she did hear something. A steady, insistent beeping. Then another beep joined in with the first one, louder. Closer.

Her mind was still sluggish from the climaxes, so it took her a second before the beeping penetrated. Oliver got there first. "The smoke alarms!"

"The cookies!"

Seven

Renee scrambled off his lap and grabbed her top, but Oliver didn't even bother with clothes. He went streaking out of the bedroom at a dead run, his legs still a little wobbly from the sex.

Dear God, if she burned the whole damned house down...

He went skidding into the kitchen. For the second night in a row, smoke was curling out of the oven and hanging in a low cloud against the ceiling—but no flames. Thank God for that.

Oliver moved fast. He grabbed the oven mitts and turned the oven off before he snatched the cookie sheet out of the oven. Still no flames. Just carbonized cookies. Again.

These smelled even worse than the ones from last night. He didn't want to dump them in the sink and there were still dozens of cookies covering every flat surface.

Thankfully, Renee came running into the kitchen. "Door!" he barked, the oven mitts getting hotter the longer he held on to the cookie sheet.

Coughing, Renee turned and ran. Oliver had to wonder where the hell she was going—there was a perfectly fine door on the other side of the island that opened onto the backyard, but then she yelled, "The pond!"

Right—water would be good. Oliver's hands were growing dangerously hot despite the oven mitts so he took off after her.

She jerked the front door open and stood to the side while he ran outside and barreled straight into the pond. With a silent apology to Fred and Wilma, he threw the whole damn mess into the water before tearing off the oven mitts and letting them fall to the water. He bent over and let the water cover his hands. It wasn't cold because the day had been sunny and warm but compared to the hot cookie sheet, the water felt amazing.

A few yards away, the cookie sheet hit the water with a sizzle, as if he'd been forging iron. He looked up to see the whole thing floating, the hockey pucks formerly known as cookies still smoking.

On the far side of the pond, Fred and Wilma made a lot of noise and flapped their wings in displeasure at having their evening swim disrupted.

"Tell me about it," he muttered, turning his attention back to his palms. They were red but not burned. He didn't see any blisters forming, nor any white skin that signaled a severe burn.

He dunked his hands back in the water, just to be sure.

He heard a strangled noise behind him and he looked over his shoulder. Renee was standing a few feet up the bank. She'd managed to grab her T-shirt and it hung down to the top of her hips, the hem fluttering in the breeze. Backlit by the setting sun, he could see every inch of her silhouette outlined and that was when his brain chose to remember that, less than ten minutes ago, he'd been inside her, feeling the shocks of her body releasing a climax upon his.

But something wasn't right. Her hands covered her mouth, her eyes were huge and her shoulders were shaking. It about broke his heart to see her like that.

They were just cookies. It wasn't like she'd burned the house down or scarred him for life. He didn't like her looking so fragile, so scared.

But then she asked, "Are you okay?" in a voice that was strangled—but it wasn't horror or misery that laced her words.

He recognized that voice. He'd heard it countless times back when they'd been kids and he and Clint had fallen for one of Renee and Chloe's pranks—he was thinking specifically of clear tape strung across his bedroom door that Oliver had walked into it so hard that he'd been knocked off his feet, tape stuck in his hair.

And Renee had stood over him then, looking almost exactly like she did right now—trying so hard not to giggle at the raging success of her trick. Trying, instead, to look worried and she'd uttered the exact same words.

She hadn't succeeded then and she wasn't succeeding now. "Are you *laughing* at me?"

"No!" she answered way too quickly. "I'm…" She took a deep breath, visibly getting herself under control. "I want to make sure your hands aren't burned."

The smoke detectors beeped from deep inside the house. Fred and Wilma continued to express their displeasure on the other side of the pond, with Pebbles and Bamm-Bamm joining in. But all he could hear was the barely contained amusement in her voice. "Fine," he said coolly, because it was the truth and he didn't want her to worry. "Just a little warm. No burns, no blisters."

"Good." Her gaze cut to his backside at the exact same moment a stiff breeze rippled over the surface of the pond. And his butt.

His bare butt. The one that was sticking straight up in the air because he was bent over at the waist. Everything was hanging *all* the way out.

"Do you think," she said, dropping her hands and trying to look serious, "that there'll be a full moon tonight?"

Holy hell, this woman. She was easily going to be the death of him, and quite possibly his house. But honestly? He was so damned relieved she was okay, that the same mischievous, hilarious Renee who'd driven him up a wall when they'd been kids was still in there that he wanted to laugh with him.

But this was Renee after all, and he wasn't about to let her off the hook that easily. Turning, he scowled at her as he walked out of the pond. "You think this is funny?"

"Maybe." She sobered and took a step back as he advanced on her. "Maybe not."

"This is the second night in a row you've nearly burned down the house, Renee. I don't think I'm going to let you bake anymore."

The light in her eyes dimmed as she paled and she crossed her arms over her stomach, almost curling into herself even though she didn't so much as bend at the waist. Shit, he'd taken it too far. He wanted to make her sweat a little but he didn't want to beat her down.

Fight back, he thought as he got nose to nose with her. *Fight for yourself.* "You, ma'am, are a menace to baked goods the world over," he intoned in the most pompous voice he possessed. "I'd even go so far as to say you're a monster to cookies everywhere, to say nothing of how you're terrorizing my kitchen, my swans and myself!"

Behind him, Fred—or maybe it was Wilma—whooped from much closer. Involuntarily, he flinched because no one wanted to be bitten on the ass—or other exposed parts—by an angry bird with a six-foot wingspan. He looked over his shoulder. The swans and cygnets had swum over to investigate the now-sinking cookie sheet, so his butt was safe. For now.

He turned back to Renee. She stared up at him, confusion written all over her face. "Did…did you just call me a cookie monster?"

"If the shoe fits." He snarled. Well, he tried to snarl. But suddenly the effort of not laughing was almost more than he could bear.

She blinked at him and then blinked again before pointedly looking at their feet. "We're not wearing shoes."

"Fine. If the shaggy blue fur and googly eyes fit, wear them!"

Fight back, Renee.

Then, miracle of miracles, she did. She gave him a fierce look and poked him in the chest. "I've got news for you, mister." *Poke.* "You're not the boss of me." *Poke.*

"Oh, yeah?" It was not the snappiest comeback he'd ever uttered.

But it did what he wanted it to do. Her eyes lit all the way back up as she smiled and then tried to scowl and frankly, she took his breath away again. This was a game. Maybe not one she'd played in a long time, but she hadn't forgotten the rules. Thank God for that. She was going to give him everything she had and that, more than the explosive sex or the questionably edible baked goods, made him feel ten feet tall. She wasn't afraid of him. He was worth the fight.

She was worth the fight. It was high time she knew it.

"Yeah!" *Poke.* "If I want to bake cookies—" *poke* "—then I'm going to bake cookies. And furthermore—" *poke* "—I'll have you know that I was doing just fine before you showed up, both nights." *Poke.*

"Ow," Oliver said, backing up a step. She wasn't poking him hard, but she was hitting the exact same spot over and over again.

"You're the reason the cookies got burned." *Poke.* "You distracted me with amazing kisses and the best sex I've ever had." *Poke.* "If you hadn't distracted me, we could be eating the perfect chocolate chip cookie right now."

Amazing kisses? The best sex? He wasn't one to brag but hell, yeah, that was good for his masculine pride. To hell with cookies. He'd have her back in bed. Or on the love seat. Hell, any semiflat surface would do just fine, as long as he could hold her in his arms and feel every inch of her body against every inch of his.

Oliver was grinning his fool head off but he didn't care. There was something so right about Renee defending herself and putting him in his place that it made him want to sing.

Sing! Him! Oliver!

He didn't burst into song. However, he did say, "Were they edible cookies?" just to drive her nuts.

It worked. "The last batch was!" *Poke.*

Stumbling backward, Oliver looked over his shoulder. The cookie sheet had sunk now, but a few hockey pucks formerly known as cookies floated on the surface of the pond. Fred and Wilma and the kids seemed mildly terrified of the things. He couldn't blame them. "The *last* batch?"

"You know what I mean—the batch before that!" *Poke.*

Oliver retreated another step. She was in fine form, his Renee. Her eyes blazed and the breeze molded the thin T-shirt to her body, highlighting her breasts and the gentle swell of her stomach and all he wanted to do was pull her into his arms and kiss the hell out of her.

"I swear to God, if I had a water balloon—" *poke* "—I'd throw it right at your head. But you know what?" *Poke.*

He grabbed her finger before she bruised him. "What?"

A victorious smile graced her face, making her look like an avenging angel. He wanted to fall to his knees and worship before her. She pulled her hand back and said, "I don't need a water balloon."

This time, she didn't poke him. She put both hands on his chest and Oliver had just leaned down to take that kiss from her lips when she shoved him. *Hard.*

He fell backward and the next thing he knew, he was sitting on his butt in the pond, wiping water from his face while Renee stood safely on the bank, staring at him.

"You…" he sputtered, wiping water from his face. The mud was squishing up his butt and around his important parts and, judging from the noise, the swans had declared DEFCON 1 behind him. "You pushed me!"

For a second, she looked just as shocked as he felt. Then her face cracked into a huge smile and it was like the sun breaking through clouds after days of endless rain.

"You. Pushed. Me," he said in his most dangerous growl and then he splashed as much water as he humanly could at her. He missed, of course. From this angle, he could see under the hem of her long T-shirt and, as she danced out of the way of the water, he caught glimpses of her bare body that made him hard all over again, despite the mud.

She laughed, loud and free, and clapped her hands in delight. "Don't move," she giggled, pointing. "I'm going to get my phone. I think Chloe needs to see a picture of this—the high-and-mighty Oliver Lawrence stuck in the mud!"

"The hell you will," he said, trying to get to his feet. But the mud was slippery and he lost his balance and splashed back down again. He couldn't even keep a straight face this time.

The sound of her happiness was worth it, he decided. He'd be cleaning mud out of his crack for a week but he'd take the fall for her again, just to hear her laugh as if she didn't have a care in the world. She wrapped her arms around her waist and bent forward, tears of joy rolling down her cheeks.

"You win this round," he yelled, aiming for his best

villain voice—high-pitched and nasal. "But I'll be back!"

Then, just like she always had years ago, Renee jammed her thumbs against the side of her head, waggled her fingers at him and stuck out her tongue, yelling, "*Nyah, nyah na nyah*, you can't catch me!" before she spun on her heels and bolted back to the house. Her legs flashed in the dim light, her bottom peeking out from under the shirt with every step she took.

All he could do was watch her go, an unfamiliar lightness settling around him even as the sun sank behind the house and shrouded the pond in shadows. He hadn't felt this lightness back when they were kids. She'd driven him nuts and he'd done everything he could've to return the favor. But now?

They weren't kids anymore. Life had changed them both but he could still give her those moments of joy.

"Are you coming?" she yelled from the front door.

He rolled onto his hands and knees and made sure he had his feet under him before he stood. Pond water sheeted down his body, leaving muddy rivulets all across his legs. "Hell, yeah," he called back.

Because she wasn't going anywhere without him.

Eight

"These aren't bad," Oliver said around his sixth attempt to eat one of Renee's cookies.

"Really?" Renee ducked her head, a delicate blush pinking her cheeks. "That was the last batch. That survived anyway."

He wanted to cup her blushing cheek in his palm and kiss her again and again. But then again, earlier he'd wanted to pull her back upstairs and try out a few other positions with her, but he couldn't.

Just like always, Oliver had bowed to the demands of reality. Stupid reality.

Frankly, he was lucky he hadn't mooned half of Mineola. Because that's about how many people had suddenly appeared on his property.

While Oliver had been splashing in the pond and doing everything in his power to make Renee laugh and fight back, his housekeeper, Lucille, had called three times to see if the house was on fire or not. When she couldn't get ahold of anyone at the house, she'd called the fire department. The fire trucks had shown up about five minutes after he'd got his naked butt back inside the house, with Lucille hot on their tail. And then she'd scolded Oliver like he was a schoolboy and demanded to know why he'd installed a houseguest without telling her because she could have brought over some more food.

"Or at least some better desserts," Lucille had grumbled when she'd got a good look at the kitchen.

But Oliver had introduced Lucille to Renee and, after her initial shock, Lucille seemed to be warming up. She picked up a cookie from a different batch and took a small nibble. "Good heavens, you're not supposed to use that much salt!"

"Well, I figured that out," Renee said defensively—but at least she said it with a smile. "Eventually. Why would anyone label *teaspoon* and *tablespoon* so similarly?"

Lucille gave Renee a look that made it clear the older woman didn't know if Renee was joking or not.

Oliver snagged another edible cookie and handed it over to Lucille. "The important thing is she figured it out."

Lucille was not one for effusive praise, but even she nodded and said, "That's not half bad," which made

Renee bust out another one of those luminous smiles. "Honey, I can teach you to bake, if you'd like." She eyed the mess again. "Might be easier. Or at least safer. When are you due, honey?"

"Oh." Renee turned a pretty pink and stared down at her belly. Oliver couldn't figure out if she was embarrassed by this question or not. "September 27."

Because of course she knew the exact date of conception. The day her husband took his own life. Oliver didn't like the way Renee seemed to pull back into herself. He shot Lucille a look that he hoped communicated *say something nice*.

And Lucille, bless her heart, did. She wasn't a grandmother of six for nothing. "Pregnancy suits you," she announced a tad too loudly.

"It does?" Clearly, Renee didn't believe her.

"You've got that glow, honey. Some women look tired or drained, but you?" She waved her hand near Renee's belly. "Some women were born to this. You're one of them, you lucky duck."

Renee looked doubtfully down at her stomach. "But I'm fat."

Lucille looked truly insulted by this. She patted Renee on the arm. "Oh, honey—who told you that? They were nothing but jealous. You're gorgeous." She turned a hard stare to Oliver. "Isn't she?" It was not a question.

"I already told her that. Multiple times—because it's true," he replied, watching Renee's cheeks color even more. Which meant he almost missed the look Lucille gave him, one that had him realizing that he might have overplayed his hand.

Thus far, he and Renee had attempted to stick with their original story—they were childhood friends and he'd given Renee free use of his ranch while she was hiding and he was working in Dallas.

But that story wasn't holding water, so to speak, and Oliver knew it. It was the middle of the workweek and yet he was at Red Oak Hill. And not only was he at Red Oak Hill, he'd also barely got out of the shower and got pants on before the place had been crawling with firefighters. At least Renee had located her leggings. They'd told the fire crew that he'd fallen into the pond trying to deal with the carbonized cookies—which, again, was true.

But it wasn't a huge leap to get from him naked in the shower to him naked with Renee. He'd even caught two firefighters nudging each other with their elbows and winking at Oliver's story.

Yeah, no one was buying that half-truth here. Worse, he'd screwed up and used Renee's real name when he'd introduced her to Lucille within earshot of at least three firefighters and now there was no going back.

For all intents and purposes, Renee's presence at Red Oak Hill was now common knowledge.

Especially because Lucille was no idiot and it was clear Oliver had screwed up again. Damn it. This was all going wrong. Lucille, he trusted, but the firefighters? And now Lucille was giving him The Look?

To avoid Lucille's sharp gaze, Oliver snatched up another cookie and immediately regretted it. Coughing, he spit the too-salty one into the trash. "I think we can get rid of these," he sputtered, scraping the whole batch off the cooling rack and directly into the trash. "We're lucky no one else tried these."

"*You* were lucky you weren't caught with your britches down," Lucille said, dumping another batch into the trash and stacking the dirty dishes in the sink.

Oliver froze, the blood draining from his face. A quick glance at Renee told him that the opposite was true for her. She was turning an unnatural shade of scarlet. She shot him a helpless look.

Oliver wanted to bolt but he couldn't abandon Renee to Lucille's questioning. "You should ask Lucille for some tips," he said, ignoring the status of his britches. "She does most of the cooking for me. And she makes an amazing cinnamon roll. I know it's not a cookie but…"

Bless her heart, Lucille said, "You should try a sugar cookie, honey. Once you get the basic dough recipe down, then you can start messing around with it."

"I saw some recipes but they looked really complicated—lots of detailed icing," Renee replied. "I don't think I could do that."

"You only need that much icing if you've got a boring

cookie." The older woman eyed the kitchen counters. "I don't think anything you bake could ever be boring."

Oliver could have kissed the woman. Renee looked relieved and that was the most important thing. "I did see some really cute things on Pinterest I wanted to try…"

And they were off. "I'll be in my study—Bailey is emailing me," Oliver mumbled, making a break for it. He didn't know if it was a lie or not. Bailey probably *had* been emailing him.

He dropped into the chair and put his elbows on his desk. He was tempted to yank his hair out of his head, if only to make sure he hadn't hallucinated the last two hours. Renee was right. None of this—the smoke alarms, the fire department, Lucille—would've happened if he'd been able to stick with the plan. He should've stayed in Dallas. Barring that, he should've kept his hands off her. And barring that…

He shouldn't have teased her in the pond. But he hadn't been able to help himself. A jumble of emotions churned in his chest. He wasn't thinking straight and he knew it.

He wanted Renee. One time with her wasn't going to be enough. If anything, he wanted her more now than he had before he'd stripped her bare and slid into her body.

He did not want her to burn his house down. Thus far, they'd had two close calls and he didn't want to find out if the third time would be the charm.

He needed to make her laugh again, to see that joy

lighting up her face. He didn't want to see the shadows that hovered around her anymore.

And he'd completely failed her because people knew where she was now.

What a freaking mess.

So he did what he always did when things went sideways on him. He worked. He logged in and attacked the twenty-one emails that Bailey had sent him since 3:45 p.m. this afternoon with a fervor that bordered on possessed. He sent a message to Herb Ritter that he absolutely would make their 9:00 a.m. tomorrow morning. He reviewed the messages from Chloe summarizing how negotiations with ESPN were going. He ignored the ones from his father.

"Oliver?"

He jumped. How much time had passed? It wasn't enough. Seeing Renee in the doorway to the study, her head tilted to the side, light from the hallway settling around her shoulders—he was terrified to realize it might never be enough. "How's everything going?"

"Good. Really good." She stepped into the room, but not very far. He could feel the distance between them. "Lucille's going to bring over some recipes on Friday. I helped her with the dishes. There's a right way and a wrong way to wash dishes, apparently."

He knew that, but he said, "Who knew?" in a teasing tone.

She took another small step into the study. "I'm

going to go take a shower. For some odd reason, I smell a little like a pond and charcoal."

"Do you now?" Oliver couldn't fight back the grin.

She nodded, putting together a reasonable appearance of innocence. "Will you..." She paused and straightened her shoulders, her chin coming up. Oliver didn't like that look on her. But he was starting to recognize it for what it was—Renee putting her armor on. "Will you be here when I get out of the shower?"

Screw this distance. Oliver was out of his chair before he could think better of it, crossing the room and pulling her into his arms. "I won't leave you without saying goodbye."

That wasn't what he wanted to say. Hell, he didn't know what he wanted to say. It wasn't like he was going to tell her he loved her. He cared for her, yes. He worried about her. He wanted her happy and well and safe. But that wasn't love.

The problem was, he didn't know what it was.

She looked at him, her eyes round with something that looked too much like fear. "Is this goodbye?"

This was *not* love. But it was definitely something more intense, more focused than he was used to feeling.

"No," he said, brushing his lips over hers. "It's not."

She exhaled against his mouth and he deepened the kiss, clutching her tighter so that her body was pressed against his chest. His hands moved down her back, cupping her bottom and pulling her against him. She gasped as the hard length of his arousal made contact with the soft flesh under her belly.

He lost himself in her. That's what this was. It wasn't love and it wasn't lust. He was simply lost to her.

God help him, he didn't ever want to be found.

He already had her shirt half-off when a loud clatter echoed from the kitchen, followed by some of Lucille's more creative language. Oliver and Renee broke apart, both breathing hard.

"I…" Blushing furiously, Renee backed away. "I need to shower."

Oliver begged to disagree. What she needed was to stay right here in his arms. Preferably with less clothing between them. But he didn't say that out loud. He needed to put more space between them. He needed to get his thoughts—and his dick—back under control. Hell, he needed to drive back to Dallas tonight so he could meet with Herb Ritter in the morning.

But he just might need Renee more.

So all he said was "Sounds good," as if that could've even begun to make things right.

He wouldn't have thought it possible but Renee blushed even more. "Okay."

"Good," he repeated dumbly, his arms beginning to shake with the effort of holding them at his side. But he fought those baser urges because the moment his control slipped, he'd do something foolish like pull her back into his arms and tell her to wait because he was absolutely going to join her in the shower. And then the bed. And everywhere in between.

With a smile, she turned and fled. It wasn't until he heard her steps overhead and the door to her bedroom shut that he exhaled and staggered back to his desk on weak knees.

"She's something." Lucille's gravelly voice made him jump again. "I like her."

Oliver pulled himself to attention. "Sorry about the kitchen. We, uh, lost a cookie sheet to the pond." He was real proud of the way his voice was level. Strong. Less...*shaken*.

Sitting in front of the desk, Lucille stared at him long enough that Oliver began to shift uncomfortably. Like the swans, the older woman had come with the house. She had been cleaning Red Oak Hill for almost twenty years. It had only made sense to keep her on when Oliver had bought the place six years ago.

He'd run a background check on her and got to know her, of course. He wasn't stupid. But the fact was, Lucille was so good at maintaining Red Oak Hill to Oliver's standards that he paid for her to come to Dallas one day a week and clean his condo, as well. And because he valued loyalty, he paid her well.

He was just about to open his mouth and tell her not to mention anything about Renee to anyone, but she beat him to the punch. "That's the Preston Pyramid Princess, right?"

"Right." He could feel himself deflating. "She was

best friends with my sister when we were growing up. Her brother was my best friend. They were practically family."

"Darn shame about her husband. He shot his fool head off, right?"

"Right. She's had a rough go of it since then. I'm just giving her a place to lie low for a bit."

"That girl reminds me of me," Lucille announced.

"Really?" Lucille had three kids by three different fathers, but Dale was only her second husband.

Lucille gave him a smile that made it clear she knew what he was thinking. "Different circumstances, same story. Like recognizes like. I love my kids and I love my grandkids. I'm not saying I'd want to change anything because all of it—the good and the bad—gave me them. But I'm an old woman now."

"Hardly," he muttered. Lucille was all of fifty-five.

She ignored that interruption. "I can look back with a little distance. I had a rough childhood—my mom wasn't around much and my dad was a mean drunk. I spent years doing whatever the hell I wanted because who was going to stop me? No one. At least, that's what I told myself."

Okay, so maybe a picture was slowly starting to emerge of a less-than-happy childhood for Renee. But that wasn't anything comparable to what Lucille was talking about. However, discretion was the better part of valor, so Oliver kept his mouth shut.

Lucille went on, "But I didn't know what I wanted.

I'd meet someone and suddenly, whatever they wanted was what I wanted. Drugs, alcohol, sex—did I ever really want any of that? Or did I just go along with it because I needed the approval? Who knows, if I'd met Dale earlier…" She let that trail off, her gaze getting soft.

He was about to argue with this assessment of Renee—but then he remembered something she'd said about her wedding. She would have been perfectly happy with something small and intimate but she'd wound up with something like ten bridesmaids and custom-engraved crystal and it was all wildly over-the-top.

Was that what Lucille was talking about? Hell, he didn't know. "As nice a guy as Dale is, I don't think he's Renee's type."

He didn't expect Lucille to scowl. "Do you know why she's been destroying my kitchen? Because she's trying to figure out what she wants. Not what her father, or I assume her mother, wants, not what her husband was willing to give her. Not even what you want, Oliver Lawrence. What *she* wants."

"Is that supposed to be difficult?" He didn't mean to sound flippant. But he didn't see how this was some sort of lifelong struggle. Okay, Renee was still in her midtwenties. And she was going through a rough time in her life. But most people got a handle on life by the time they got out of college.

After all, he knew what he wanted. He wanted to

leave Lawrence Energies and his family behind and get back to his real life in New York and...

Didn't he?

Lucille leveled a look at him that, if he'd been a younger man, would have made him drop his head in shame. As it was, he had to look away. "If you spent your entire life being told that what you want is useless and worthless," she said in a tone that walked a fine line between understanding and disappointed, "that what makes you happy is stupid, then yeah, it's difficult."

"I don't think she's stupid." In fact, he knew she wasn't. God knew he didn't tolerate fools. She was bright and charming and vivacious and gorgeous and... he wanted her.

"You know she's not stupid. I know she's not stupid. But does she know that?"

"Of course she does. Why wouldn't she?" But even as he said it, he had to wonder.

She *did* know, didn't she? That Oliver thought she was all of those amazing, wonderful things? That he never considered her stupid or worthless, not even back when they'd been children tormenting each other? She might've been a pain in his backside, but he had always known that she was smart and talented.

Lucille stood. "She can't stay here. Too many of those boys recognized her."

"You're the one who promised you'd teach her how to bake." The idea of sticking Renee in some soulless hotel

where she wasn't allowed to wander around or even attempt a simple sugar cookie left him feeling vaguely ill.

"It's going to take me at least a day to put that kitchen
back in order," Lucille grumbled, but she smiled as she
said it. "Take her to your condo. I'll be there on Monday anyway. The building has decent security. They
won't be able to sneak up on her like they would here."

Oliver had been worried about reporters but what if
someone heard that the Preston Pyramid Princess was
here and decided to take matters into their own hands?
What if someone came here looking not for a scoop,
but for revenge? "You raise a valid point."

Lucille smirked. "Good. Tell her I'll see her Monday." She headed for the door but paused and looked
back at him, a knowing smile on her face. "Besides,
that would save you a lot of driving."

Yeah, Oliver wasn't fooling anyone.

"Tell her I'll bring my grandma's snickerdoodle recipe," Lucille called over her shoulder and then the door
opened and shut.

Oliver dropped his head into his hands, trying to get
a handle on the jumble of thoughts all clamoring to be
heard inside his mind at the same time.

What did she want? What did he want? Well, he
knew the answer to that.

He wanted to go upstairs and sweep Renee into his
arms and fall into bed and spend the next twelve to
twenty-four hours forgetting about cookies and firefighters and housekeepers and scams and family. He

wanted to revel in her body and show her how good he could be for her. He wanted her with a fierceness that was a little frightening, if he were being honest.

Did she want him? Or did she want what he wanted?

He shook his head. None of that mattered, because neither of them was going to get what they wanted. Instead, they were going to get what they needed and right now that was to leave the seclusion of Red Oak Hill and head back to the anonymity of Dallas.

This was a problem. If word got out that Renee was here, then the only reasonable conclusion would be that Renee was with him. Even if she were safely tucked away in his condo, people might still try to get to her. And they might try to get to her *through* him.

He wanted to join her in the shower but he couldn't risk being caught with his pants down for the second time in one night, so instead he composed an email to Bailey, updating him on the change in circumstances and directing him to order extra security for the condo and the office. Then, when Oliver had gauged enough time had passed that Renee was probably at least partially dressed, he went upstairs to break the news to her.

Damn it all to hell.

His father was going to find out sooner or later.

Oliver prayed it wasn't sooner.

Nine

This was not how she'd planned on spending her evening—making a late-night mad dash back to Dallas for the safety of Oliver's condo.

It wasn't like Red Oak Hill was hers. She'd spent the equivalent of a long weekend there. But she was sadder than she wanted to admit to leave it behind. She been able to breathe there and even though she was a born-and-bred city girl and should be relieved to be back in a big city, she wasn't.

It was true it was easier to hide in the city. But she hadn't had to hide for a few days. She'd been able to sit on the porch and take a walk around the pond and be herself. No worries about who was going to get a terrible photo, no thoughts as to what the next headline would be. Just…peace.

If only she hadn't ruined that.

"Did you enjoy baking the cookies?"

Renee turned her attention back to Oliver. His gaze was focused on traffic. She didn't recognize where they were, but it wasn't like she'd spent a lot of time driving around. She'd had a taxi take her from the airport to Oliver's office. That was all she knew of Dallas. "I did. There was something soothing about mixing up the ingredients and hoping for the best. And when they were awful, I could try again."

God, she sounded pathetic. But that was the truth. Wasn't that why she'd come to Dallas and to Oliver? All she could do right now was mix things up and hope for the best.

She braced herself for a cutting comment, an affirmation that she wasn't capable of anything other than a Pinterest fail, a warning that cookies would make her fat—something. Oliver couldn't be happy that his house smelled burned. He couldn't be thrilled about bringing her to yet another home on such short notice. He couldn't enjoy the way she kept upending his life again and again.

So when he reached over and lifted her hand to his lips, pressing a tender kiss to her palm, her mouth fell open in surprise. "Then bake cookies. I won't distract you anymore."

Then he kissed her hand again. Sweet warmth

spread from where his lips touched her bare skin and she wanted to revel in it.

Because underneath the worry and anxiety that had become her constant companion in the last few months was something new.

She and Oliver had made love. No, that felt too soft to describe what they'd done. They'd had hot, sweet, block-out-the-rest-of-the-world sex that had been a gift because he'd made her feel amazing and then, when it was over, he'd asked if she needed more. Because he was willing to give her more.

Oh, how she wanted to take him up on that offer. She'd wanted him to come upstairs and climb into the shower with her and pick up right where they'd left off before the fire department had shown up.

Instead, they were back in Dallas and any of those hot, sweet feelings had been put aside in the name of practicality.

"In fact," Oliver went on, "we should have a new rule—the moment we feel *distracted*, we have to turn off the oven before anything else happens."

Anything else? Did he mean wild, crazily satisfying sex, or did he mean an actual, full-fledged fire breaking out? Because it would've been tragic enough burning down Red Oak. It would be horrific to set fire to a high-rise building that housed hundreds of other people.

Good heavens, what would the press do to her *then*?

But that was the moment when Oliver tugged on her hand and suddenly his lips were skimming over the delicate skin of her wrists. "Or maybe you should just turn the oven off the moment I walk in the door. Just to be sure," he murmured and even though it'd been a long day, heat still flooded her body.

"Oh. Okay. Good plan." Renee knew she should say something grateful or appreciative. But there was a lump in her throat that made breathing, much less talking, difficult.

With a final nip at her skin, Oliver lowered her hand and laced his fingers with hers. "I can't promise that things won't get even crazier and there are certain realities we can't overlook. But I want you to be comfortable. If there's something you want to try, somewhere you want to go—tell me. I'll do my best to make it happen. Because I want you to be happy, Renee."

She took a long, slow breath. It wouldn't do to burst into heaving sobs at that, even though it was one of the most beautiful things anyone had ever said to her. She was going to blame the hormones for all of this tearfulness.

On the other hand…what had that meant, if there was something she wanted to try? Were they talking about baking or…

Surely he wasn't talking about her fantasies. They were already making excellent headway on them. The knight in shining armor riding to her rescue? Yeah, that alone covered a lot of territory.

But before she could come up with any sort of reasonable response, she was saved by Oliver withdrawing his hand and turning into an underground garage. "We're here."

As he entered the access code and parked in his assigned spot, Renee felt old doubts creeping in. Oliver was being wonderful—there was no question about that. In fact, before he had come upstairs to tell her she was coming back to Dallas with him tonight and her baking lessons were being postponed because she wasn't safe at Red Oak Hill anymore—before all of that, she had been having the most wonderful day she could remember.

And it wasn't just the cookies.

She could *not* remember the last time she'd had a conversation with anyone that didn't involve the phrase "You should…" in one way or another.

Because everyone had an opinion. Of course her lawyers were going to say that—she was going into debt for their legal advice. But her parents? Her brother? Her husband? Her friends? It was for the best. Wasn't that what they all said? No one had said it louder than her mother. Her *suggestions* were thinly veiled orders she expected to be followed.

When was the last time anyone had asked her what she wanted? Promised to make it happen? When was the last time anyone had gone *this* far out of the way for her?

When was the last time someone had done something as simple as make her laugh? Because she couldn't remember laughing as hard as she had at the sight of Oliver, butt naked, jumping out of the water while a pair of perturbed swans made menacing noises. For as long as she lived, she would never forget the sound of Oliver's laughter when he'd landed on his butt in the pond. And there'd been that moment when she'd thought he was furious that she'd nearly ruined everything—and instead he'd been teasing her.

Cookie monster, indeed.

She'd stood up for herself. She'd laughed so hard she'd got a stitch in her side. She'd come out on top— literally, she'd come on top of him. When was the last time she'd enjoyed sex so much?

Today had been magical. She hadn't climaxed like that in so long that she had almost forgotten what it was like. And then, instead of telling her she was getting fat, Lucille had told her that she had a glow about her. That she would get better at cookies if she kept practicing.

She hoped that, one day, she'd get back out to Red Oak Hill. Back out to that place out of time where she could be free, even if it were just another short visit.

Carrying her bag, Oliver led her toward a private elevator that required a key code to open. "The security here is good. The lobby is open, but all of the elevators are coded and guards are on duty twenty-four hours a day. No one should be able to slip in."

She nodded as the doors closed behind them. This was important information—necessary, she was sure. But she didn't want to hear about safety and privacy because that was a constant reminder that she was the pregnant Preston Pyramid Princess and her family had hurt people and, even if she wasn't responsible, she was still at fault.

Her stomach lurched as the elevator began to climb. It'd been easy this evening to forget that simple truth that Oliver was risking not just his home but his reputation and his entire business by protecting her. It wasn't ruined cookies that drove Oliver out of his ranch house tonight. It was her.

Now he was bringing her here? This was a terrible idea. Why couldn't he see that she was a risk to him?

But he couldn't. "I'll request that you not leave the building without me. I know you can handle yourself, but I don't want to worry." He cupped her face in his palm. "I'm..." He took a deep breath. "I'm not used to worrying. I don't like it."

She leaned into his touch. "I'm sorry." Sorry for making him worry, sorry for setting off smoke alarms, sorry for upending his life. She was sorry for things that hadn't even happened yet but were still highly likely to occur.

"Don't apologize." His voice was deep as he lifted her face. "Not to me," he said against her lips.

She shouldn't lean into the kiss. She shouldn't want him and she certainly shouldn't take what he was offering. If she had half a brain, she would catch a ride to a nice hotel and spend the next week or so ordering room service and watching television. If she watched enough Food Network, she'd probably learn a lot about cookies.

But she didn't want to. It was selfish and greedy, but

she wanted to kiss a man who wanted her—only her. So she did. She wanted to wrap her arms around his waist and pull him against her so that her breasts were pressed against his hard chest, so she did that, too. And when the elevator dinged to a stop and the doors opened, she didn't want to end the kiss.

But she had to when Oliver pulled away from her, his eyes dark with desire. "We should get inside," he said, but he didn't let her go. He slid his free arm around her waist and guided her down a short hallway with only three doors. "My condo is half the floor. Of the other two condos, one is an oil baron who only sleeps here when he's in town on a business meeting and the other family, I believe, is summering in Paris. So the only people who come off the elevator should be me or Lucille."

She suppressed a sigh. "All right." Like Oliver had said—there were certain realities that neither one of them could ignore. Oh, how she wanted to ignore them.

Wouldn't it be lovely to pretend that they were coming home after an evening out, just the two of them? That this was an everyday occurrence, kissing on the elevator and struggling to keep their hands to themselves until they were behind closed doors? Oh, how she wished that this were her real life instead of a brief, wonderful interlude.

He'd said that all she had to do was ask and he would do his best to give it to her. Somehow, she didn't think he'd been talking about the rest of their lives.

Because she couldn't ask that of him. Sooner or later, her family's scandal would catch up with her. Even if nothing came up about their misadventure with the fire department today, eventually word would get out. That was just the nature of scandals. She'd be called back to New York to testify, kicking off a fresh round of gossip and hatred, especially because she was more noticeably pregnant every single day. When that happened, it wouldn't be just her caught in the cross fire. It would be Oliver.

She shouldn't have barged into his life. If she were smart, she'd bail now.

But then he opened the door to his condo and ushered her inside. When the lights came on, she gasped. "It's beautiful."

The apartment she had lived in with Chet had been worth close to six million, but in reality it had been a smallish two-bedroom apartment. Chet had hated it, hated that they hadn't been able to get the place he'd really wanted, which had gone for ten million and had four bedrooms and a formal dining room. Renee had always considered their snug condo to be perfect and she'd known that, sooner or later, they would move out. But that had never been good enough for Chet. He hadn't looked at it as a starter home. He'd looked at the smallish condo with only four windows and no balcony and seen nothing but failure because it wasn't the very best.

Renee had always feared that he'd had the same feeling when he'd looked at her.

But Oliver's place? There were floor-to-ceiling windows that wrapped around a wall behind a dining table set for six and continued around the corner to another full wall of windows with plush leather sofas and chairs that was interrupted only by an elaborate fireplace and mantel. She glanced around, but she saw no signs that this place was occupied by more than one person.

The place looked…lived-in. Like his study out at Red Oak Hill. Everything in here was of the highest quality. She knew an expensive Persian rug when she saw one and there were three scattered around with various seats grouped around them. All that wealth was understated.

This was his home, on the top floor of a thirty-story building with a view that encompassed half of Texas.

Nothing could touch her here. No other windows looked down into his apartment because this was the tallest building for blocks. She was above the fray here—literally. "You can see for forever," she said in a sigh, drifting to a window and staring out at the twinkling lights of the city. It wasn't as perfect as Fred and Wilma swimming in the pond but it was *amazing*.

Oliver came up behind her. Her breath caught in her chest when she saw the look in his eyes. Even the hazy reflection in the window couldn't blur away the desire in his eyes. And she was still in her leggings and a T-shirt. After everything that had happened today—and especially with her looking like she did—how could he still look at her like that?

"The view is always spectacular," he said as his

gaze dipped to her chest. Her nipples hardened to tight points and she heard him suck in a deep breath. Then he stepped into her and rested his hands on her shoulders. "But it's even better now."

Oliver watched Renee's reflection in the glass as he rubbed her shoulders. He should be giving her a tour of the rest of the condo. He should be showing her to the guest room and giving her plenty of space. It was late and they'd had a crazy afternoon and she was pregnant and…and…

And none of it mattered when he touched her. Despite the air-conditioning and her clothes, he could feel her body's warmth under his touch. When she leaned back into him?

Yeah, this was what being lost felt like.

He wrapped his arms around her waist. "Tell me what you want, babe. I want to give it to you."

Her reflection smiled a saucy smile at him and reached up to lace her fingers into his hair. He went hard for her, harder than he'd ever been in his life. Which was saying something, considering it'd only been a few hours since he'd buried himself in her body.

"I don't want to talk about safety and security," she said, giving his hair a tug to pull him down to her.

"Done." He didn't want to deal with those realities anymore, either. He had her here now and he sure as hell wasn't going to let her go.

"I want to make cookies tomorrow."

He slipped his hands underneath her T-shirt. Bless these loose shirts and doubly bless her for going without a bra. Did she know how much it tortured him to watch her walk around, her beautiful breasts swinging freely? "I'll show you where the fire extinguisher is before I leave for work," he said, cupping her in his hands and stroking the undersides of her breasts.

She inhaled sharply, but he didn't want to rush this. Earlier, he hadn't been able to hold back, to hell with the consequences. But now? They had the rest of the night. If he was dragging at his meeting with Ritter tomorrow, that was a price he was willing to pay. As long as he had Renee in his arms tonight.

So he took his time fondling her breasts and teasing her nipples. He focused on listening to her breaths and watching her reactions in the glass.

When her body bucked in response to his gentle tug on her nipples, he felt it down to his toes. When she moaned as he rolled those nipples between his thumb and forefinger, he moaned with her. He couldn't help it. Her pleasure was his.

She was his.

"Look at you," Oliver breathed as he stared at Renee's reflection in the window. Her mouth was open as she panted, her eyes heavy-lidded. It had almost killed him to watch the light in her eyes die a little when, instead of taking her right back to bed, he'd told her they were leaving.

He wanted to see the Renee who managed to get the

upper hand on him, who laughed at his corny jokes, who wasn't afraid of anything—she was the Renee he wanted back. He'd do anything to make her smile again.

The moment the thought crossed his brain, he was stunned by the truth of it.

He would do anything for her.

"You feel so wonderful," he told her as he let the full weight of her breasts fill his palms. "But I need to see these. I need to see all of you."

She inhaled sharply as he skimmed his hands down her ribs and over her hips to the hem of her T-shirt. But when he started to lift, she stopped his hands. "I don't... What if someone sees?"

"No one can see in these windows. That's one of the reasons I've bought this condo."

She didn't let him strip off her shirt. If anything, her grip on his hands tightened. "But..."

Oliver dragged his attention away from the reflection of her chest in the window and looked at her face. The sensual glaze of desire was gone, leaving her face drawn and tight. Then, somewhere far in the distance, a light blinked. It was probably a helicopter or something that was at least a few miles away, but Renee gasped as if someone had flown a drone into the window and started snapping pictures.

Right.

He kissed the side of her neck and then bent over, sweeping her legs out from under her. "Oliver!" she squeaked in alarm.

"I'm being a terrible host," he said, holding her tight against his chest. "I haven't even given you the tour yet."

"Oh?" She relaxed into him, her arms going around his neck. "I saw the living room."

"But not the kitchen," he said, walking right past the doorway on his left.

"It's lovely," she murmured and then her lips were against his neck. "I look forward to spending time there."

"Office," he ground out through gritted teeth as he carried her past the dark doorway on his right.

"It suits you perfectly," she agreed without looking. Then she began to suck.

His knees almost gave. "Guest room." Another fifteen steps—he could make it.

"Is that where I'm staying?" Her teeth skimmed over his skin with the barest hint of pressure.

Take what you need, he wanted to tell her. Hell, he wanted to shout it. "No," he groaned, all but staggering into his master suite. Dimly, he was aware this was supposed to be a slow, steady seduction where all the focus was on her. "For as long as you want, you're staying here with me."

"I…"

"Tell me," he all but begged. His body was on fire for hers but he didn't want to presume a single damned thing. "Tell me what you want."

She leaned back and gave him that smile, the exact same grin she'd launched at him seconds before she'd shoved him into the pond. It made him want to yell with victory.

"I want you." Then she bit him—not hard, but it sent a jolt of need through him unlike anything he'd ever experienced before.

He couldn't even make it to the bed along the far wall. He all but dropped her in front of the door to his walk-in closet.

The door covered with a full-length mirror.

He paused only long enough to reach over and flip on the light. The drapes were pulled and no one would be able to see anything he did to her.

And he was going to do it all.

When the lights flickered on, she gasped. But he was already pulling her T-shirt over her head. "God, Renee," he whispered, starting where he'd left off at her breasts. This time, he tugged on her nipples a little harder and was rewarded with a shudder. "You truly take my breath away."

"I do?"

It just about broke his heart to hear the doubt in her voice. She truly didn't see it.

This was a problem—but he had the solution. He'd make her believe she was the most beautiful woman he'd ever seen or he'd die trying. And given how much he was aching for her, she might be the death of him.

With the last of his control, he spun her around. For the second time today, he hooked his fingers into her pants and pulled, baring her. "Do you have any idea what you do to me?" Because the sight of her bottom begging for his touch really was going to kill him.

So he touched. He slid his hands down her full hips and then to her backside, where he dug his fingers into her generous flesh. She shuddered at his touch. Good. "I'm…I'm getting an idea."

"Not good enough. You need to know how badly I want you."

But when he looked in the mirror, he could see her struggling. "Oliver…"

"Babe." It was rude to interrupt her but he could see that she was going to do something terrible, like ask if they could turn the lights off and hide under the covers and he couldn't let her think that there was a single thing about her he didn't want. "Watch," he commanded, falling to his knees so he could skim his teeth over the soft skin of her bottom. "Watch what you do to me. Watch what I do to you." Then he bit her. Not hard enough to bruise. He'd never hurt her. But he needed her to stop thinking and start feeling.

It worked. She sucked in a ragged gasp as he kissed the sting away and slid his hand between her legs.

Slow. He needed to take this slow. Because…reasons. Good ones, he was pretty sure.

But those reasons were lost to him as Renee shifted her legs apart for him. She put her hands on the mirror, her gaze moving from Oliver to where he was touching her and back again. He could see her surrendering to her needs—her eyes growing darker, her chest heaving as her breath came faster and faster.

He dug deep for words that were more than just *mine*. "Do you see how pretty you are?" he asked quietly, kissing his way up her back. "Do you see how luscious you are?" He cupped her bottom and squeezed. "God, I love your body."

"Even though…"

If she was trying to convince him that he couldn't want her because someone had told her she was fat, he was going to lose it.

He surged to his feet. "Renee. *Look*." He gripped her by the chin—again, gently—and turned her face so she had no choice but to look in the mirror. "I don't care what anyone else says. I only see you. I see your beautiful eyes and your delicate collarbone," he said, letting his hand drift down to that bit of skin. "And your breasts. God, your breasts." He cupped them again. Since he couldn't kiss them from this angle, he settled for kissing her neck—which he did without breaking eye contact in the mirror. "You are the sexiest woman I've ever seen."

"Don't tease," she said but at the very least, it came out as a breathy sigh. "I'm sorry I pushed you in the pond."

"I'm not." That moment when she'd fought for herself had been glorious.

That was what she needed to do right now—fight for herself. "This is the only way I'd tease you, darling." He slid one hand over the swell of her stomach again and down between her legs. "God, do you see how pretty you are? See how your eyes darken with want?"

"Yes," she moaned, her head dropping back on his shoulder. But she didn't look away as he tormented her nipples, her sex.

He thrust his hips against her backside, his erection chafing behind his pants. "Do you feel what you do to me?" This was where they'd been earlier at the window before she'd allowed doubt to crowd out desire. She sagged against him, bearing down on his hand, but he wrapped his free arm around her waist and held her up. "Look at you," he said, breathing hard as he stared at where he was touching her. "Look at us."

"Oliver," she said, her voice straining.

He pulled back only long enough to shove his pants aside. "Feel what you do to me?" he moaned against her skin.

Then she reached back and circled him with her hands. When she gripped him tightly, he had to brace himself against the mirror to keep from falling to his knees again. "Who else gets you like this?"

"You. Only you."

Her hand slipped lower to cup him. "No wife? No mistress or…" She squeezed and he made a noise that might be considered undignified, but he didn't give a single damn. "Or a girlfriend?"

He shook his head, trying to think. But what she was doing to him—there was no thinking. "Nine months—

no, eight. Eight months since my last lady friend." Her grip shifted again and he was helpless to do anything but thrust into her hands.

"What am I, Oliver?" Her voice was so soft that he had to look at her. "What am I to you?"

Not a wife, obviously. But the moment that thought crossed his mind, he had to close his eyes against it.

He'd never wanted to get married. Never wanted to bring someone into his messy family life. He had enough responsibilities—how could he add a wife or children to managing his father and running Lawrence Energies and, who could forget, the damned rodeo? How much more did he have to give, when there was so little of himself left over?

But Renee was already a part of his family. She had been for years.

"Am I your mistress?" she went on and he heard an edge to her voice, one that made him want to weep with joy.

She was fighting back.

"No," he ground out when she gave him an extra-firm squeeze. Not that he wanted to think about her cheating, lying ex right now, but he realized on a fundamental level that she had to make sure. "Not a mistress. Not a… Oh, God," he groaned as she stroked him. "Not a girlfriend, either." That wasn't a strong enough word for what she meant to him.

"Then what am I?" Her voice was quiet but there

was no mistaking it—she had him in the palm of her hand. Literally.

When she reached back with her other hand, Oliver's restraint cracked. He grabbed her by the wrists. "I can't wait," he growled as he pushed her hands against the mirror. "Don't move."

He grabbed the condom from his pants and frantically ripped it open. He nudged her legs apart and then slid into her warmth with one long thrust. They both moaned.

Mine. It was all he could think as he grabbed Renee by the hips and buried himself in her over and over again. It wasn't slow or sweet or tender. The way he took her was raw and hard and heaven help him, he loved it.

She loved it. Her hands on the mirror, she bent forward at the waist and thrust her backside up and out, just enough that she could see his face unobstructed in the mirror. And holding her gaze while he furiously pumped into her body was the singularly most erotic thing he'd experienced in his life.

She moaned and then shouted, "Oh, God—Oliver!"

"Renee," he growled, digging his fingers into her skin, fighting the urge to mark her as his.

She pushed back into his thrusts and cried out, her muscles clenching him so tightly that he couldn't hold anything back. Not with her. She would always push him past the point of reason, past the cold grip of logic.

He needed to do something. Something romantic, like whisper sweet words of promise in her ear. Something practical, like *take care of the condom. Something*, for God's sake.

"You destroy me, Renee" was what he came up with. "You simply destroy me."

Because Renee Preston-Willoughby had walked into his office and thrown everything ordered and planned about his life right out the window. His organized days of meetings? Gone. His long-term plans to grow Lawrence Energies—including the damned rodeo? Cast aside. His careful management of his family? Forgotten. His promise to his mother that he'd keep the family together? A distant memory.

All that was left was this fierce need to be with Renee and protect her—and her unborn child.

The destruction was complete.

Because she was his, by God. And he was not letting her go.

Ten

Renee focused on keeping her breath steady and even. Okay, it was a little heavy because sex with Oliver was proving to be so much *more* than she was used to.

That man had scandalously stood her in front of a mirror and made her believe—really believe—that she was pretty and desirable and worth the risk. He was worried about her and he wanted and needed her and he couldn't keep his hands off her and it was perfect.

Or it had been, right until he'd ruined it.

Oh, she knew he hadn't meant it as an insult or even a warning. But there was no mistaking that "you destroy me" for what it was—the truth.

Because she would. Sooner or later, she would ruin him. Not on purpose. Never on purpose. But it was inevitable, wasn't it? Either she was going to do something accidental, like set fire to one or more of his homes, or word would get out about their connection and his reputation would be dragged through the mud.

Knowing her luck, probably both. He thought he understood her messed-up family. But even if things went perfectly from here on out—the press left her alone or her baby's delivery was textbook or Oliver continued to be wonderful?

Her family would go on trial or her mother would find some way to ruin everything all the way from France because there was no way Rebecca Preston would approve of what Renee was doing. Preparing food? Doing the menial work of washing dishes? Doing something unladylike like pushing a friend into a pond and laughing out loud?

She hoped no one from that fire department went to the press. If her mother could find a way to ruin the little bit of peace Renee was struggling to hold on to, she would. Just out of spite.

She and Oliver were fogging the mirror up with their breaths. She didn't want to move. She wanted to pretend like everything was fine.

But she was tired of that, too. She'd spent years pretending and she wasn't going to anymore. At least, she was going to try to not do it as much. She might have to ease into this whole total-honesty thing.

But she definitely wasn't going to let thoughts of her mother into this room. Rebecca Preston had abandoned

Renee long before she'd decamped to Paris. It was high time Renee returned the favor.

She pushed against the mirror and thankfully, Oliver backed up. She shivered from the loss of his body covering hers.

She turned to go to the bathroom just in case she fell apart, but Oliver caught her hand.

"Will you stay with me tonight?"

The smart thing to do would be to say no. He had a guest room. She was a guest.

But then he added, "It's whatever you want," and her resolve buckled because honestly, she wanted to spend the night curled in his arms. Whatever this was, it would end badly for all parties involved—she didn't have any doubt about that.

But the fact was it was going to end badly no matter what. Maybe it was selfish and definitely shortsighted, but she wanted to hold on to this little bit of happiness while she could.

So she brushed her lips against his and said, "I'll stay," because he'd done everything in his power to protect her. He'd made her feel good again. For heaven's sake, he hadn't even been that upset about the ruined cookies.

By the time she finished in the bathroom, Oliver had carried her bag in. "You're going to need more clothes," he said absentmindedly as he stared at the solitary piece of her luggage.

She didn't exactly have the money for new things, so she said, "It's not a big deal. I can do laundry."

Actually, she wasn't sure she could but that had to be one of those things that came with instructions. At the very least, Lucille should be able to walk her through the process while minimizing fire hazards.

Oliver looked up at her like she might be crazy. He must've taken advantage of the other bathroom because, while he had taken off his button-up shirt, he was still in his trousers and undershirt and she was completely nude. There was no missing the appreciative gleam in his eye but she was suddenly tired and feeling self-conscious. Her hands dropped to her thighs, covering the scars, but she thought she did so casually enough that he hadn't noticed.

If he wasn't naked, she wasn't going to parade about. The nightstand on the right side of his bed had the alarm clock, so she walked around to the other side and slid under the covers. She immediately felt better.

"You're just going to walk around braless? What happens when you need to leave the house?"

That was a good question. Suddenly, she had a feeling that Oliver was going to insist that she allow him to buy her clothes.

Because that's who Oliver was. If he saw a problem, he was honor-bound to find a solution. She had enough clothes for a week—but in another few weeks, she'd be pushing her luck with the underwear. She had a month, tops, in her yoga pants. Maybe another month in her loose tunic tops. And Oliver was right—eventually, she'd need a bra again. But if anyone caught wind of Oliver buying maternity clothes…

Destroyed. That was the only word for it.

To distract him, she arranged herself on the bed in what she hoped was an inviting way, making sure to suck in her stomach while the sheet fell down off her hips—but stayed above the scars on her thighs. "I thought you requested I not leave."

"You're not Rapunzel. I'm not going to lock you in a tower." His eyes darkened as he looked her over. "Although it's damned tempting to keep you all to myself for the weekend, at least."

Tempting. She liked that. She could still be tempting. And she could have him all to herself for the next few days. "What was that about the weekend?"

He made a noise that was part growl, part groan and all need. But then he paused. "Can I get you anything before I join you? Water? A snack?"

And that, in a nutshell, was why she was in Oliver's bed. "Just you."

She didn't have to ask twice. He flung his clothing off and was between the sheets within moments. When he pulled her against his chest and pressed a kiss to her forehead that would've been tender if there hadn't been so much heat packed into it, Renee sighed with pleasure. As soon as she settled in his arms, though, her eyes began to drift closed. It had been a very *long* day…

When Oliver spoke, she startled back awake. "I have

to go to work tomorrow and Friday," he said apologetically. "I've put this meeting off twice and there's no avoiding it. By Sunday we should know if anyone has connected you to Red Oak Hill. If not, I'd like to take you out. We've got museums or movies or the theater or—"

"Gosh, like a real city?" she couldn't help quipping. She ruined the sarcasm by yawning, however.

"Smart-ass." But as he said it, he began to stroke her hair. "There's a pretty park with a pond and ducks about a block away—we can just take a walk. Although I wouldn't recommend that at high noon, unless you enjoy sweating. Whatever you want—I'm yours for the weekend."

"I'll think about it." She was too damned tired to make any sort of decision right now. It was probably for the best that Oliver was going to work tomorrow. Today had been wild on about six different levels and she needed to recover.

But...there was something she wanted to do before Saturday. "Would it be all right if I called Chloe tomorrow?" So much had happened in the last week—which was saying something, because a lot had happened in the last five months. If she vented to Oliver, she knew he'd listen—but she also knew that he'd try to solve the problem. And she didn't want to be his problem.

She really needed a girlfriend, which meant Chloe. Frankly, there wasn't anyone else.

She felt the tension ripple through Oliver but as

quickly as it had appeared, it was gone. "I don't see why not. I'm sure if you explain the situation, she'll keep your whereabouts quiet. And she's launching a new clothing line, so she might be able to help with the clothes."

She smiled against his skin. Even when he wasn't solving the problem, he was still solving the problem. Men. *This* man.

Mine, her brain whispered as she yawned again. She was his and he was hers...wasn't he?

"I'll call her. But I won't tell her about us," she murmured against his chest. She wished Chloe were here, although...if she were, there would be no hiding the fact that Renee and Oliver were sleeping together. Or they were going to, shortly. Very shortly.

As she drifted off to sleep, she thought she heard him whisper, "I doubt that'll make much of a difference."

"You're *where*?" Chloe Lawrence squealed in Renee's ear.

"At Oliver's condo." Renee thought it best to leave out any mention of Oliver's ranch house. "It's a really long story, but I needed a place to lie low and you're... Where are you?"

"Omaha." Then Chloe's voice got muffled and Renee got the feeling she was giving instructions to someone. "Sorry. Oliver has given me a lot more control over the rodeo—which is great. But it's a lot of responsibility and combined with the Princess clothing launch..."

Renee exhaled in relief. "Which was exactly why I didn't try to track you down. I figured I would just hang out here until you came to Dallas and then we could catch up."

There was a long pause. "I told you not to marry that asshole."

"You were the only one," Renee said, trying to keep the bitterness out of her voice and failing. It wasn't Chloe's fault she'd been right—or that Renee hadn't listened. She deserved that *I told you so*. And probably a few others.

"Oliver would've told you not to marry him, too," Chloe said, because even as a kid, she'd never been able to let anything go.

Because this was a telephone call and not a video call, Renee rolled her eyes. "Tell me about the clothing line." Nothing like a change of subject to dance around the Oliver issue. "Couture or cowgirl?"

"Cowgirl," Chloe said so firmly that Renee had to wonder if she was insulted by the couture suggestion. "Why?"

So Renee laid it all out as quickly as she could. It was odd that Chloe was more up-to-date on the situation than Oliver had been. But she knew of Chet Willoughby's suicide—she'd sent flowers. She knew about the pyramid scheme and had sent emails—not a lot, but some—offering Renee support and help if she needed it.

What she didn't know was how the prosecutors had seized anything that was even remotely close to an asset.

"So all of the designer clothes are gone and even if I still had them, they wouldn't fit. I'm pregnant. I only brought two bras with me and neither works anymore." The words *your brother doesn't seem to mind* danced right up to the tip of Renee's tongue, but she bit down on them before they could escape. "Nothing's going to fit in a few weeks and I might be here longer than that."

"Man, I long for the days when I can wear nothing but yoga pants," Chloe said with a sigh. "But I understand the problem. I bet it's driving Oliver nuts that you're not in a suit or something. I hope he's not being a total butthead."

"He's…fine." Which was not a lie. He certainly wasn't being a butthead. But that left a lot of room around what *fine* meant. "It's not like anyone will see me in his condo."

"Wait—why did he take you to the condo? Why didn't he take you to the ranch?"

Renee bit her lip. "He did. But I decided I wanted to bake cookies and there was…an incident. The fire department showed up."

"Did you burn Red Oak Hill down?" Chloe asked in a panic. "He loves that place! And those stupid swans!"

"No, no." Although just thinking about it—again—made her stomach flip. "It was only some cookies. The swans are fine. It was just smoke."

Unexpectedly, Chloe began to laugh. "Was Oliver mad? He's *such* a stick-in-the-mud."

That was the thing Renee kept coming back to—he

had been upset. But he hadn't taken it out on her. Instead, he'd treated it more like she'd pulled off a successful, funny prank and he was impressed. She told Chloe the whole story.

Chloe hooted with laughter. "I would've paid good money to see that. I knew he was hiding something! If he'd told me you were there, I would've tried to get there, even if only for the day."

"Yeah? I'll admit, it'd be great to see you." Of course, Chloe was too smart by half. She'd take one look at Renee and know for sure that she was sleeping with Oliver. "But Oliver's taking care of me. So you don't have to worry."

Chloe made a humming noise and Renee realized she might have overplayed her hand. But then Chloe said, "Hey, the rodeo is coming to Dallas—well, Fort Worth, which is practically the same thing—in three weeks. I'll be in town for at least five days—longer if I can swing it. You, my friend, are going to spend a few days with me and we are going to catch up. I'm going to take you to the rodeo," Chloe said in a tone of voice that made it clear this was nonnegotiable. "A pitcher of sangria, unhealthy snacks and—"

"I'm pregnant." As if anyone could forget that small detail.

"I don't mind. That's more sangria for me." She was quiet for a moment. "Renee, are you sure you're doing okay? I know Oliver can be grumpy. And rude. And bossy. And—"

"It's fine," Renee interrupted. True, Oliver could be all of those things. But far more often, he was encouraging and kind. When he teased her, she could tease right back and feel safe that, instead of telling her she was wrong, he'd laugh with her instead. "And are you sure going to a rodeo is the best idea? I'm supposed to be lying low."

"It'll be fine! I'll send you some Princess clothes to tide you over but when we're at my place, we'll try everything on. We'll get you a fab hat and I'll tell Oliver to keep an eye on you." She sighed heavily. "As long as we keep you away from Flash, it'll be fine."

"Well…" She remembered Flash being an extremely irritating little brother. There had been lizards involved. But maybe he'd changed. After all, she wasn't the same little sister she'd been back then, either. "I'd actually love to go to one. I've never seen the Princess of the Rodeo in all her glory." Chloe snorted. "But only if Oliver agrees…" She was pretty sure he wouldn't.

"Oh, he will," Chloe said, sounding way too pleased with herself. "It's his damned rodeo, too. He doesn't appreciate how awesome it is. If we're lucky, Flash will get stepped on by a bull. But," she went on, apparently cheered by that thought, "in the meantime, try not to kill him. I know he's uptight but it's just because he never has fun."

"He doesn't?" The man who owned a pair of swans named after the Flintstones seemed like he had maybe a little fun at least some of the time.

"He wouldn't know fun if it bit him on the butt."

Renee smiled at the memory of Oliver jumping when the swans took offense to his invasion of their pond.

Chloe went on, "I worry about the butthead. All he does is work and micromanage. He argues with Dad constantly about the business. He orders me to keep Flash out of trouble—as if anyone could keep Flash out of trouble," she added under her breath. "And all he does with Flash is fight. Promise me you won't let him boss you around."

Renee let that thought roll around her head. If she hadn't spent the last few days with Oliver, she would've agreed with Chloe's assessment. Because that's who Oliver had been, at least in her memory.

Frankly, that was who he'd been at her brother's wedding and that'd been five years ago. Because she'd tried. She'd struck up a conversation with him and she would've asked him to dance, if she'd got to before he'd had so much to drink. Oliver hadn't tried to boss her around, but he had been the textbook definition of *grumpy*.

"He's been great," she finally said, hoping that wasn't giving too much away. "Really, I don't want you to worry about us. I'm more concerned about what to wear to your rodeo."

There was a moment when she didn't think Chloe was going to go for that subject change. But then she said, "What size are you?" And they fell into the familiar habit of discussing clothes and sizing.

"I'll send some samples out for you," Chloe said. "It's not what you'd normally wear, but you'll blend in. And they're *samples*. You can't pay me for them," she added.

Because Chloe was a real friend, bless her heart. It shouldn't feel different, accepting this gift instead of one from Oliver. But it did. "Thanks, Chloe. I can't wait to see you in a few weeks."

"If Oliver gives you any trouble, call me immediately."

Renee almost defended Oliver again, but she decided that would only make Chloe more suspicious so instead she said, "I will. Promise."

She sat there for a moment after the call ended. Chloe's clothing line didn't make maternity clothing, but she was going to send things a size or two up, which would give Renee a couple of more months to figure out how she was going to afford everything else she needed. Which meant the only thing she needed to buy on her own was underwear, and she could afford a bra and a few pairs of panties.

She began to browse on her phone. But instead of basic white or nude underthings, she found herself looking at pretty bra and pantie sets. Because Oliver wanted to take her out and show her the town. But more than that, because *she* wanted to feel pretty. Leggings were great but they weren't doing much for her ability to look in a mirror and feel good about what she saw. She wanted to be *tempting*, damn it. And she had about two hundred dollars left in her bank account from the money the feds had allotted her to travel with. New panties it was.

She still heard her mother's voice, dripping with icy menace as she complained about Renee getting fat. But at least now, she also had the memory of Oliver telling her how gorgeous she was and how he couldn't keep his hands off her.

She had to choose who to believe. And her mother had never loved her.

Not that Oliver loved her. Of course not. He liked her and he worried about her and that...that was enough.

This whole situation was still a mess. Just like her life. But she couldn't stop thinking about what Chloe had said—Oliver never had any fun. That picture of him didn't mesh with him laughing and naked in the mud, or of him insisting that he show her the town.

It was high time they both started having more fun.

Eleven

"**A**re you sleeping with her?"

It took a lot of work to make sure Oliver's face didn't react to this bald statement. Obviously, Renee had talked to Chloe. He'd known there was no way Chloe wouldn't put two and two together. But he hadn't quite expected her to scream it in his ear. "One moment." He turned to Herb Ritter, praying the older man hadn't been able to make out Chloe's screech. "Thanks again for coming by. I'm sorry our meeting had to be pushed back."

The older man did something Oliver never would've seen coming in million years—he winked. "I hope she was worth it," Herb said in his gravelly voice. "But try not to let it happen again."

Oliver came *this close* to asking Herb to keep the

revelation that a woman was involved to himself, but he managed to hold on to his tongue. At this point, he was neither confirming nor denying anything involving Renee to anyone.

Including his own sister. He waited until the door had closed behind Herb before he turned his attention back to his sister, who was humming the *Jeopardy!* theme song on the other end of the line. "Can I help you with something?"

"You are! You're sleeping with Renee! I *knew* it."

Was there anything worse than a little sister gloating? If so, Oliver couldn't think of what that might be. But he had all the plausible deniability in the world when Renee was the subject. "What are you talking about?" Maybe he'd missed his calling in the theater.

"She told me you were being nice to her and frankly, you're not nice to anyone. Especially not her. So clearly you and Renee have hooked up."

He knew better than to fall for the trick of making a blanket denial. Chloe had missed her calling as a lawyer. Instead, he focused on the first part of the accusation. "I am perfectly capable of being polite, as is Renee. We both grew up and are no longer whiny children. Unlike some people I know," he said, hoping that Chloe would take the bait.

She didn't. "Do you have any idea how big of a mess she's in? And you creeping up on her isn't helping anything! You should keep your damn hands off her! Just because she's vulnerable and needy doesn't give you the right—"

"Stop right there," Oliver growled and, to Chloe's credit, she did. "First off, I am not taking advantage of anyone. Second off, I know exactly how big of a mess she's—I spoke with Clint, the ass, over the phone."

"Really? *Whoa*."

He ignored her. "Third off, whatever happens between consenting adults is absolutely no business of yours—"

"I knew it," Chloe muttered under her breath.

"And fourth off," he ground out through gritted teeth, "she is *not* vulnerable and needy. She is not a helpless damsel in distress or a lost child and it's insulting her to imply she is. She's a woman in a difficult situation doing the best she can to get her life back on track for her and her child and all I'm doing is giving her the space to decide what she wants to do and helping her accomplish those goals, whether it's attempting a cookie recipe or shielding her from the press. And furthermore," he went on, because he was on a roll and Chloe wasn't interrupting him and that was a rare thing, "I am not creeping on anyone. *Really*, Chloe? You know damn good and well that Mom loved Renee like she was one of the family and all I'm doing for her is what I'd do for you or Flash."

Except for the part where he stripped her down and lost himself in her body. But again—he was neither confirming nor denying that.

"Because that's what Mom would want and expect out of me—out of all of us. So don't insult me or Renee, *sis*, because she's had quite enough unfounded accusations and rumors to last her the rest of her life. Are we clear?"

There was a stunned moment of silence. Oliver wasn't sure if the stunned part was coming from him or from Chloe.

Because he might have just lost his temper. There may have been shouting involved—he wasn't sure. Hopefully, Herb had got out of earshot.

"Is Renee why you gave me the negotiations?" All of her righteous anger was gone.

Yes. But he kept that to himself. "The rodeo is yours, you know that. Just because Dad doesn't appreciate all the work you do to make it profitable doesn't mean I don't."

"Did you just compliment me?" Chloe let out a low whistle. "You did! Jesus, she's good for you. And before you yell at me again, I'm not insulting either of you."

He growled.

"There's the brother I know and love. Listen, I invited Renee to stay with me when I'm in town and I'm taking her to the rodeo."

"That is *not* a good idea." But even as he said it—all right, even as he *growled* it—he knew he was being ridiculous. Hadn't he offered to take her to museums and theaters and whatever she wanted? A rodeo wasn't that different, was it?

Then again, it was the rodeo. Ugh.

"Keep your pants on. I'm sending her a bunch of clothes and we'll find a hat. I could give her big hair. Ooh! We'll try new eye makeup. Trust me, when I'm done with her, no one will recognize her."

He would. He'd recognize her in a crowd in the middle of the night.

"Oliver? You know I wouldn't do anything to hurt her. Or you, I guess."

"Thanks, brat." But he let go of the breath he'd been holding all the same. "How are the negotiations coming along?"

The conversation thankfully veered off into business then, but Oliver couldn't get Renee out of his mind. When he ended the call, he couldn't do anything but sit there and stare at the pictures lining the far wall—all those artistic action shots of the rodeo that Renee had noticed the moment she'd waltzed into his office.

He hated the rodeo—the smells and dirt, the bulls, the young idiots who risked life and limb for a belt buckle—and that absolutely included Flash. Oliver hated the whole damned thing. But if Renee wanted to go see one and Chloe could disguise her appearance… maybe they could pull it off.

He had so much he needed to do. He should have Bailey order some flowers—delivered to the office so that he could give them to Renee in person. And more baking things—he'd make sure Lucille brought plenty of supplies with her. He needed to find out who Renee's lawyers were and make sure they were doing their job. And he should get the name of a trustworthy doctor. He didn't know how long she'd be here, but if there was a problem, he didn't want to take her to the emergency room and hope no one recognized her. A private doctor who would be on call—for a price, of course—was the solution. And…

Well, she'd be here at least long enough to go to the rodeo in three weeks. And after that?

A vision of her rounding out with her pregnancy materialized in his mind. She absolutely glowed, damn it, and he had a powerful urge to tell her she wasn't going anywhere until after the baby was born. But it wasn't like she could just up and relocate with a newborn. She'd need help then, too. And that baby—Oliver would have to make sure that the media didn't descend like locusts and turn that innocent child into nothing but clickbait.

Would she want him to be there when the baby was born? Would she want him by her side, holding her hand and telling her how amazing she was? Would she want him to hold that whole new person that was the best of her? Or…not?

A sickening wave of loss twisted his insides at the thought of Renee giving birth without anyone beside her to fight for her and that baby. Even if it wasn't him, at least he could make sure Chloe was there. Just so long as Renee knew she wasn't alone.

He shook his head. He was getting ahead of himself by months. *Years*. Doctors and lawyers were all well and good, but it wasn't like he was asking Renee to stay forever. Chloe was right about that, at least. Renee's life was too complicated for anyone to be thinking about anything more long-term. There were still trials and plea deals to work through and the media to avoid. He needed to focus on the next three weeks. After that, he'd focus on the next three weeks.

Right. He needed roses and chocolate chips. And more condoms. But those he was getting himself. Because, while he trusted Bailey completely, there was no way in hell Oliver was asking anyone else to pick up protection.

Because that's all this was. He was protecting Renee, damn it.

And if that meant he had to go to the rodeo, then he'd suck it up.

For her. Only for her.

"Can I ask you a question?"

Breathing hard, Renee managed to open one eye and peer up at him. "I'm going to need five minutes to recover," she wheezed. The man was simply the best—and most intense—lover she'd ever had.

At least this time they'd made it to his bed. There was something to be said for actual sheets and pillows. Plus, the air was scented with roses and the smell of them together.

He'd brought her flowers. It was a ridiculously sweet

thing and if she thought about it too much, she might get teary.

He grinned. "Not that." Moving slow, he skimmed the sheet down her body. At first, Renee thought he was going for another seduction—right until he unveiled the scars. "These."

Renee's lungs seized up. How could she have thought that he wouldn't notice them? Oliver was the most attentive, thoughtful and observant man she'd ever know.

But old habits died hard. She felt her chin lift and her shoulders square, which was impressive considering she was sprawled out over at least three of the four pillows on the bed. "These what?"

"Renee," he said, giving her a look. "Don't do that."

"Do what?" But even as the words left her mouth, she winced. Stupid defense mechanisms.

"*That.* When you put on your armor. You don't have to do that with me. And these are…weird." He looked at her thighs, catching her hands before she could cover them. "I thought they were freckles but they're too regularly spaced and all grouped together. And your right leg has a lot more of them."

How, exactly, did someone say, *Oh, those? That's just what happens when you repeatedly jab a fork into human skin. What of it?* She had no idea.

But if she said, *I don't want to talk about them,* then Oliver would wonder. And he'd ask again. He wouldn't take the pat answer at face value because he was the rare man who actually wanted the truth instead of pretty little lies.

And she didn't want to lie to him. She wanted there to be truth and trust between them.

Funny how those things were easier said than done.

Then he leaned down and pressed a kiss to the rows of tiny scars. "You don't have to tell me, if you don't want. But if you change your mind, I'll be here."

Really, the man was too perfect. She exhaled slowly and then, when she was sure her hand wasn't shaking, ran her fingers through his hair. "All right."

He rested his head on her leg, staring up at her with something that sure seemed like adoration. She was just happy he could still see around her belly. Honestly, between the pregnancy and the cookies, she was impressed she hadn't got bigger than she already had. "Do you want to go to the rodeo?"

"Maybe." She relaxed back into the pillows and stroked his hair. "But you hate the rodeo."

He grinned and she almost wished she could take a picture to show Chloe and say, *See? He can have fun.* "I can be mildly inconvenienced for an evening if you want to see the Princess of the Rodeo in action," he said as he moved to lie down by her side again. She couldn't help but think he sounded resigned to the fact. "Who knows—maybe we'll get lucky and Flash will get stepped on."

She burst out laughing.

He notched an eyebrow at her. "What?"

"Chloe said the same thing. I'm sensing a theme."

"It'll be fine. We won't be in the stands—there's usually a separate seating section for the VIPs," he said, stroking a finger down her cheek. "Brooke Bonner is the musical act that night, too. We'll make a date of it. If you want."

She thought about that. "It can't be any riskier than going to a museum, right? And I do like Brooke's music. Country rockabilly or whatever—it's good girl power music."

"Then we'll go." He squeezed her tight.

Her heart ached with a strange sort of happiness. It was such an unusual feeling, knowing that someone was willing to do something they didn't want to just for her.

She curled back against his side. "Oh, I ordered a few things today to go with the clothing Chloe's sending."

"Hmm?"

"A new bra. And matching panties."

Oliver groaned, which made her laugh again.

She hadn't been able to spend the money on her usual brand—La Perla was not cheap. But she'd found some cute sets at a discount site for less than fifty dollars, which was as much as she could comfortably spend. Then she'd done her best to guess on sizes, erring on the side of caution. If they were too big right now, they'd fit eventually.

"I can't wait to see them."

"Well, you'll get to do that before me—I didn't know the address here so I had them sent to your office." It wasn't like she couldn't have found out the street address of this condo. But there was something to be said for upping their pranks to a more mature level. One that included a lingerie delivery to the office.

Oliver rolled onto her, pinning her beneath his weight. The man was amazing—five minutes really was all he needed. She giggled as they struggled to get the sheet out from between their bodies.

Then, holding himself over her, his smile faded and was replaced by a look of such intensity that it took her breath away all over again. "God, Renee, you destroy me," he said before he captured her lips with his and it was a good thing he was kissing her because she didn't know what to say to that.

Oh, what a mess. She couldn't bring herself to tell him about the scars, about why she and Clint had always been at the Lawrence house instead of their own. But the longer she kept quiet, the more he'd feel like she hadn't put her faith in him when he did find out.

And the longer this not-dating thing they were doing went on, the more time he spent with her, the bigger the implosion would be. She knew all of that and, sadly, she was too selfish to put a stop to it.

Because Oliver was the best thing that had happened to her in a long, long time. So she kissed him back and wrapped her legs around his waist and, after he rolled on the condom and plunged into her, she dug her fingers into his bottom to urge him on because she wanted him.

She might not ruin him. Not like she'd been ruined.

But his personal life would become public fodder and his business would take a hit. Because of her. Because of *this*.

But at least he knew it.

Hopefully he'd never find out about the rest.

After two and a half weeks of playing house, Renee was more than ready for a change of scenery.

Not that she was complaining. She'd managed to produce not just a decent chocolate chip cookie on a consistent basis, but had also turned out surprisingly edible sugar cookies and even a batch of snickerdoodles. She was giving Lucille a solid 75 percent of the credit for that, but still. Oliver was taking cookies to work to share with his staff on an almost-daily basis. She had no idea how he was explaining that, but no one had died of food poisoning so it must be okay.

The amount of satisfaction she felt when she opened the oven and pulled out a sheet of nearly perfectly round cookies that not only looked right but tasted good was amazing. Even better was when Oliver came home and, after a kiss—okay, sometimes after a lot more than kissing—he'd try a cookie and tell her it was good. The first time he'd pronounced a snickerdoodle she'd made all by herself "really good," she was so happy she'd actually started crying.

Stupid hormones.

The day he'd brought home the underthings she'd ordered, they never made it to the cookies. Hell, they didn't even make it to the bedroom—not at first anyway. The only time Oliver had hesitated was to ask if the oven was off.

It was.

The day the box of clothes arrived from Chloe, Renee spent the whole afternoon playing dress up and video chatting with Chloe about what worked and what didn't, what Renee liked, what she might change. She got two tunic tops that might last her a few months and two pairs of super-skinny-leg jeans two sizes larger than she normally wore that fitted comfortably with the addition of a rhinestone belt. Chloe had even included a pair of boots—*because everyone wears them and you should break them in now*, she'd said.

Which is how Oliver came home one night to find her in boots and not much else.

They barely made it to the hallway that night.

She baked and learned how to wash dishes and do laundry and clean up after herself. She pestered Lucille for information about babies and pregnancy and also how to vacuum when the older woman came every Monday to clean the condo. Renee watched baking shows and kids' cartoons and whatever else struck her fancy, including a kung fu movie with subtitles.

And when Oliver came home from work, they had fun together. There hadn't been any breathless updates on the Preston Pyramid Princess being spotted in Texas so Renee didn't dread leaving the house. They went to late showings of movies and picked up carryout food—she'd never eaten so much barbecue in her entire life but it was glorious—and when she announced that maybe she'd like to learn how to crochet, he took her to a craft store.

He didn't ask about the scars again and she didn't tell him. But then again, he didn't ask about her former husband or her family and she wasn't about to taint their time together by bringing any of that crap up. She was surprisingly, amazingly happy right now. If only they could stay this way.

It wouldn't last. It couldn't. Renee knew this like she knew her name. The way she burned for Oliver was something white-hot and clear—but, like all raging infernos, it would burn itself out soon enough. After all, she'd once believed that Chet loved her beyond distraction, and see how that had turned out?

She knew Oliver wasn't the same kind of person Chet had been. She *knew* that. But it was hard to unlearn a lifetime of lessons. A few really great weeks didn't change things, not in the long term. Her family was still toxic and she might be called back to New York City at any moment and there was still a pregnancy to deal with. She had no idea how long she and Oliver could share a bed and a condo before things got awkward and even less of an idea of where she would go when it did. She couldn't imagine him relishing the idea of a crying newborn upending his world.

But that was months off. Right now, things were good.

And in a few days, Chloe was coming.

Then they were all going to the rodeo.

Twelve

He wasn't wearing a hat and that was final.

Oliver had no problem putting on the boots and the belt buckle, and jeans and a button-up shirt with a sports jacket were fine, but he drew the line at a hat. Yes, Flash looked decent enough in his black felt hat but Oliver was of the opinion—the correct opinion—that his father looked like a life-size Howdy Doody doll in his enormous Stetson.

No hats.

Oliver was fully aware he was being irrational. But he had barely seen Renee for the last few days. When Chloe had blown into town like a twister, she'd swept Renee up and together they'd decamped to Chloe's place for "quality girl time."

Which was fine. He was perfectly capable of entertaining himself. He'd been doing it for years.

But when he came home to an empty condo and no fresh-baked cookies, it bothered him and it had nothing to do with actual cookies. Renee wasn't there to breathlessly tell him about everything she'd accomplished that day. Whether it was successfully baking a loaf of bread or managing to crochet a small pot holder—at least, that's what they were calling that lopsided square of yarn—she did so with such raw joy that he couldn't help it if he wound up wrapping her in his arms before she'd even asked how his day was.

She *glowed*, damn it. Every day, her body changed a little bit and the haunted shadows under her eyes became an ever more distant memory and he was helpless to do anything but stare at her in wonder.

Because she was wonderful. And he'd missed her more than any reasonable man should miss a houseguest for the last two days.

But that was just it, wasn't it? She wasn't a houseguest, not anymore. She was...

His. She was *his*.

Wasn't she?

He was in a foul mood by the time he made it to the Fort Worth Stockyards. He was hours early, but he wanted to talk to security and make sure Renee wouldn't have any problems.

Plus, now that he was here, he was duty-bound to check in with the promoter and the stock manager about how Chloe was doing. The attendance numbers were good and her clothing line was selling well, as were the other souvenirs, but he wanted to hear it from the horse's mouth.

He gritted his teeth and grinned his way through handshakes and back slaps. Everyone had good things to say about Chloe's management, which was great.

Where the hell were she and Renee?

Then, like something out of a damned movie, the crowd of riders and horses and calves all parted and there she was. His breath caught in his throat as he stared. He barely recognized her, but he *felt* it when Renee looked up and their eyes met across the crowd. She gave him a little smile, one that sent a thrill all the way down to his toes, which were firmly wedged into his damn boots.

Chloe had worked magic on Renee. Her hair curled and artfully arranged under the brim of a straw hat, she was wearing a lot more makeup than usual. Her jeans clung to her curves and her button-up top sparkled with sequins. Her curves were more pronounced, her belly rounding out behind a ridiculous sequined buckle. He guessed that, if someone didn't know she was pregnant she might not look it. She looked like a cowgirl, one that could walk in this world.

Even though it'd only been two days, he could still see how much her body had changed and he was pissed that he'd missed a single moment.

Leading her over to where the calves for the calf-roping

event were penned up, Chloe said something to Renee and they laughed.

This was how she should always be—laughing and having fun and no doubt making cooing noises to the calf that sniffed her hand.

God, he'd missed her. Too much. He'd done his best to focus on the last three weeks instead of game planning the next few months or years, but he couldn't help the fantasy that spun out of control in his mind.

He could marry her. He could adopt her baby and they could be a family. He'd grow old with her by his side, teasing each other while eating cookies and spending long evenings in bed and doing all those things parents did with kids—parks and soccer games and school plays. All those things that his parents had done with him—and her—when they were kids.

She could make him happy.

Then a thought jolted him almost completely out of his chair. All those happy scenes?

They hadn't been in New York. They'd been in Texas, at Red Oak Hill, here in his condo. His perfect life with her was *here*. Not thousands of miles away.

Reality barged in because, in that vision of happiness, he hadn't seen his overbearing father or loose-cannon siblings or even this stupid rodeo.

Besides, he didn't even know if he could make *her* happy. She was still getting back on her feet and it probably wasn't helping that they were sleeping together. Hell, she hadn't even been able to explain those strange marks on her legs. He was afraid it had something to do with her husband, but he hadn't wanted to push. She'd tell him in her own time. He hoped. And if she didn't…

Hell.

A big man came up to Chloe and, after a second, Oliver recognized Pete Wellington. Damn it, when would he learn that the All-Stars wasn't his anymore? The last thing anyone needed right now was for Wellington to cause a scene. But if he was here—and by the look of it, giving Chloe trouble—then things were about to go sideways. Fast.

Not that Renee knew it. She looked over at him again, joy on her face. She pointed to the calf, as if to say, *See?* He shot her a thumbs-up. Her whole face lit up and damned if that didn't make him stick out his chest with pride.

He began to work his way toward her and Chloe but a rangy cowboy beat him to it. *Flash*. Damn it. He grabbed Renee's hand and kissed the back of it—then startled and stared at her face. Crap, he'd recognized her. Oliver needed to get over there before Flash did something stupid. Well, Flash always did something stupid. All Oliver could do was hope that Flash took a swing at Wellington instead of making a big to-do over Renee.

"Mr. Lawrence? I need to speak to you. Right now."

Groaning, Oliver cast a worried look at the Chloe/Pete, Renee/Flash train wreck in action before he turned. Surely they could all keep from killing each other for fifteen seconds. "Yes?"

A man glared up at him. Next to him stood a young woman with huge hair and a skintight leather skirt that was so short every single cowboy—and a few cowgirls—were staring.

"Brantley Gibbons." When Oliver blinked in confusion, the little man said, "Brooke Bonner's manager? And this is Brooke Bonner?" in a tone of voice that made it clear he thought Oliver was an idiot.

Right. The up-and-coming country singer performing after the rodeo tonight. Oliver cast another worried glance back at his siblings and Renee, but the crowds had shifted and he couldn't see them.

He put on as welcoming a smile as he could. "Yes, hello. It's a pleasure to meet you both." He shook hands. "Welcome to the All-Around All-Stars Rodeo. We're thrilled you were able to be here tonight." The man's eyes narrowed. Oliver knew that look. Something wasn't quite right. "What can I help you with?"

"For starters," Brantley Gibbons drawled, "you could see to Ms. Bonner's dressing room. We very clearly stated in the contract that there was to be—"

"Why didn't you tell me Renee was here!" This shout was accompanied by a punch to the arm that was hard enough to knock Oliver a step to the side.

"Shut up, Flash," Oliver ground out. He spun to see his annoying younger brother with his arm around Renee's shoulders and the world—well, it didn't go red. But it went a little pinkish.

Flash, being Flash, did not shut up. "How long have you been hiding her?" He sidestepped Oliver's attempt to grab him—and in the process, knocked Renee's hat off her head. "I haven't seen Renee since we were little— but maybe I should've checked her out."

"Damn it," Oliver growled, trying to step between Renee and…everyone. Because everyone was staring now. "Flash, *shut up*."

Renee tried to bend over to grab her hat, but Brooke Bonner beat her to it. "You look familiar—have we met?" the singer asked, handing the straw hat back to Renee.

Brooke's manager made an alarming noise. The look of shock on his face wasn't good. And it only got worse when he said, "You're Renee Preston, aren't you?" in a way that made the hair on the back of Oliver's neck stand straight up.

Flash launched the grin that made him a favorite with the ladies. "She was. Got herself married a few years ago?" He had the nerve to look Renee up and down. "Missed my invitation."

"Knowing you," Renee said, her smile stiffening as she cut another glance at Gibbons, "you would've used the wedding to get even for that one prank when…"

Flash held up his hands in surrender, but at least he was laughing. "God, I've missed you, Renee. You never did play fair, did you?"

The only reason Oliver didn't break his little brother's jaw was because the man between them was staring up at Renee with something Oliver wished wasn't rage—but was.

"No, she doesn't," the manager said, menace bleeding into his voice.

Renee looked at him with panic in her eyes. *Shit.* He had to get her out of here before anyone started snapping pictures. At the very least, he needed to shut Flash up.

He moved toward her as Flash went on, "Damn sorry I missed— Ow!"

Chloe beat Oliver to the punch. "Mr. Gibbons, Ms. Bonner, hello. I'm Chloe Lawrence and—" she paused to grind the heel of her boot into Flash's foot again "—we're thrilled you're here. I see you've already met Flash, one of our featured riders and, unfortunately, my brother."

"Son of a— Damn it, Chloe, get off my— *Ow!*" He shoved Chloe aside and glared. "That was unsporting of you."

Brooke Bonner giggled and Flash's head whipped around. "Hello, Ms. Bonner." With an exaggerated limp, he stepped closer, whipped off his hat and executed a perfect bow, somehow managing to get ahold of her hand and kiss it, just like he'd kissed Renee's. "Flash Lawrence, at your command."

Bonner batted her eyes at him. "Why do they call you Flash?"

If there was one thing Flash was good for, it was a

distraction. As long as his attention was on Brooke, no one but the manager was paying any attention to Renee. Oliver got between Gibbons and Renee and started backing up. Renee hooked her hand through his waistband and held on tight.

Chloe let out a long-suffering sigh. "Because that's about how long it takes for him to rub you wrong."

"Or right," Flash cut in. He still had Bonner's hand.

Another cowboy—Oliver didn't remember this kid's name—crowded up. "Brooke, baby—" But that was as far as he got before Flash had him by the shirt and shoved him back.

"You don't talk to her like that," he growled, then added in a louder voice, "None of you talk to her like that. She's a lady and you will treat her as one or I will personally make sure you live to regret it."

Normally, Oliver would be irritated by Flash's ability to make any situation about him. But he'd neatly redirected the crowd's attention away from Renee. Gibbons seemed to remember where he was. He pivoted and headed straight to Brooke's side, shooing back the crowd that had started to press in for a better view of the fight. "Brooke will not go on without—"

Oliver wasn't about to look a gift distraction in the mouth. He backed up another step and was beyond relieved when Renee followed his lead. "Chloe will be able to make everything right." She wanted the rodeo? This was her chance to prove she could handle it. Oliver gave his sister a look. "Mr. Gibbons says there's a problem with the dressing room." Chloe nodded and Oliver gave thanks he had at least one intelligent sibling.

"I'd be happy to see what I can do to make you more comfortable," Oliver heard Flash say, which was followed by something that, if Oliver had to guess, was the sound of Chloe punching their twit brother.

Oliver didn't care. He spun, tucking Renee against his side and all but dragging her away from the crowd. He glanced back over his shoulder to see Gibbons peering past people. Crap. Hopefully, Chloe would be able to communicate to Flash—either with words or fists— to keep his mouth shut about Renee if anyone asked questions.

Oliver was so busy looking over his shoulder that he nearly clocked into Pete Wellington. "Lawrence," the bigger man all but spit.

Jesus, what else could go wrong? "Not today, Wellington," Oliver growled, shouldering past the man.

"Your sister is ruining this—"

"She's in charge—take it up with her," he called over his shoulder as Renee crammed her hat back onto her head. "We're leaving."

If he'd expected her to shrink and cower, he was wrong. "Slow down."

"What?"

Still holding on to him, she pulled back, forcing him to take smaller steps. "If you run, they chase." She glanced up at him. "And for God's sake, stop scowling."

Confused, he slowed down. "Because…"

She sighed. "Because they're sharks, Oliver. If they smell blood in the water, they'll go into a frenzy." Somehow, she managed to smile up at him. "Trust me on this."

He damn near stumbled over his feet at that smile. It was warm and carefree and, if he didn't know her so well, he'd think she was just another cowgirl having a good time before the rides.

But he did know better. Her shoulders were back and her chin was up and she had every single piece of her armor locked into place. And she was right, he realized. She had a lot more experience dealing with unfriendly crowds than he did.

So he forced himself to go at a snail's pace. "I'm sorry you're going to miss the rodeo," he said, guiding her around a pair of cowboys making a beeline toward Brooke Bonner and her leather miniskirt. "I'll make it up to you, babe."

"It's fine," she lied. And it broke his heart because that lie rolled right off her tongue like he was supposed to believe that things would ever be fine again.

After what felt like a century but was probably only about ten minutes of semileisurely strolling, they made it to where he'd parked his truck. He helped her up into the cab and then fired up the engine.

Anger boiled through him. He'd told Chloe this was a bad idea, although it wasn't her fault it'd all fallen apart so quickly. No, he had Flash to thank for that. His father was going to pitch a fit over this.

For years—*years*—Oliver had kept his promise to his mother that he'd take care of the family, because Trixie Lawrence had known then that her death would devastate Milt.

She hadn't been wrong. But he'd tried and tried and *tried*, for God's sake, to be the glue that held the Lawrence family together. He'd given up on his dreams of moving back to New York and working for anyone other than his father—because that was the truth. He wasn't going back to New York as anything more than a tourist.

He'd given up so much more than that. He dealt with the damned rodeo and he ran an energy company and he didn't like either one. His whole life had been in service to the Lawrence family name. Yeah, he had money to show for that. Money was great.

But it wasn't a life.

And he wanted his life back. More to the point, he wanted a life with Renee. He wanted to make those daydreams a reality. He wanted to do what he wanted, not what was best for the bottom line or his father.

Maybe he wasn't that different from Renee, after all. He wanted her for himself.

If he lost her because of his brother, so help him God, he would not be responsible for his actions.

They were silent while he navigated through traffic, but he was thinking the whole time. He could deal with his rage and his dreams later. Right now, he had a problem—a huge one. The Preston Pyramid Princess had been confirmed at the All-Around All-Stars Rodeo by someone who'd probably lost a lot of money in the scheme.

Oliver was a man of means. He had options. He didn't have to put everything and everyone on lockdown. He didn't want Renee locked away. He wanted her to be safe—and free. And more than anything, he didn't want those two things to be a contradiction.

Once they made the roadways, he began to talk. "Here's what I'm thinking."

"Oliver…" she said softly.

He kept going. "I have a vacation home in Colorado— Vail. If I charter a flight, we could leave first thing in the morning."

"Oliver."

"But we could plant some rumors—be proactive. Say you were seen in Florida or something. I know a media specialist and—"

"Stop."

"I see the red light," he muttered as he braked. "If you're not up for flying, we can take a car, but it'll take longer. We should probably still hire the charter and send them in the other direction so—"

"Oliver." Her voice was sharp, hard. It cut through the cab of his truck like a knife. "No."

"You'd rather fly?"

"Jesus, men," she said under her breath as the light turned green. "No, I'm not going to Vail."

"That's fine. Where would you like to go? I can—"

"Are you going to make me keep interrupting you?"

He almost didn't recognize the woman next to him. There was something so cold and remote about the way she spoke, the way she held herself...

It was exactly how she'd been on that first day when she'd waltzed into his office. Had it really been a month?

One month with Renee, watching her grow and change with her pregnancy. Watching her discover who she wanted to be and making sure she had the space to be that new woman.

This was a huge problem. Because there had to be a way to keep her in his life without telling his family to go to hell or resigning. There had to be a way to get what he wanted and still honor his promises. She had to let him fix this because if she thought he was going to hang her out to dry...

"Well," she began and instead of sounding upset or even worried, she sounded...amused? "I knew this would happen."

"Babe..."

She held up a hand to cut him off. "It's fine," she repeated again. Oliver decided that the more times she said that, the less *fine* it actually was. "It was lovely while it lasted. And I did learn how to bake cookies. So that was nice."

The hair on the back of Oliver's neck stood up. He didn't like how everything had suddenly become the past tense, as if the time they'd spent together was a chapter and Renee was closing the book. "It'll be nice again," he said, hating those pitiful words. *Nice* didn't cover waking up in her arms. *Nice* didn't cover laughing with her. *Nice* didn't come close to how he felt about her. "I'll—"

"No, you won't." She all but whispered the words. And then it only got worse because she turned to him and said, "I shouldn't have come and I shouldn't have stayed. I'm sorry, Oliver."

"This is not your fault," he ground out. That did it. Flash was a dead man.

She smiled. It didn't reach her eyes. "That's sweet of you, but we both know the truth."

"The truth? What 'truth' do you think you know? Because here's the truth, Renee—if I thought it'd make things better, I'd marry you today. Right now." She went dangerously pale but otherwise, she didn't react. Oh, hell. "I'd turn this truck around and head right back to the rodeo because there's always a preacher who gives the opening prayer and I'd marry you in front of God, my crazy family and a bunch of livestock because, even though it'd be a huge scandal, it'd be the right thing to do. It doesn't matter what your father or your brother or that ass of a husband of yours did, not to me—just like I hope it doesn't matter to you that Flash is a jackass and my father is lost in his own little world and I've given years of my life trying to help them only to have them fight me on every single damned thing. I don't care about them, Renee. I only care about you."

Her eyes glimmered and her armor almost cracked. *Fight*, he wanted to yell. *Fight for us.*

"I care about you, too." He took it as a good sign that her voice wavered just a little bit. "But I can't hurt you like this."

"Like what?" He stared at her, aware that his mouth was open. "How are you hurting me, Renee?"

She turned to look out the windshield. "Did you ever wonder why Clint and I were always at your house?"

So much for that crack in her armor. "Because we were friends and our house was more fun."

Her mouth moved into something that would have been a smile if it hadn't been so damned sad looking. "Fun. That it was."

When she didn't have anything to add to that, he said, "Renee?"

"Do you know what those marks on my legs are?" she said all in a rush.

"No." He looked at her thighs as if he'd magically acquired the power to see through denim in the last five minutes.

He hadn't. But he remembered those evenly spaced dots clustered together over a few square inches of her skin. They were too perfectly spaced to be random.

"She liked forks," Renee said softly. "Whenever we did something that displeased her, she'd smile that cold smile and insist that we sit on her left side. She was left-handed. But once Clint tried to stick up for me, she stabbed him in the other leg, just because she could."

Oliver blinked and blinked again. "Those are…stab wounds?"

"The scars of them," she said with a single nod.

"Who stabbed you?" He felt an odd sort of relief that at least it hadn't been her husband.

But that relief was short-lived. "My mother, of course."

Oliver let out a slow breath. "Your mother."

Another single nod. "She had these rules. No noise, no mess, obviously. Anything that might embarrass her was not a smart thing to do."

He reached over and covered the spot on her leg about where the scars were with his hand. "I didn't know."

"We didn't talk about it," she said, as if that weren't obvious.

Another long moment passed as traffic streamed past them in the direction of the Stockyards. All those people were putting down good money to see if Flash would get stepped on by a bull or not, and to see Brooke Bonner and her leather miniskirt bring down the house. They'd buy Chloe's clothes and the men would spend money on All-Stars merchandise—all of which also had Lawrence Oil logos on it. People would buy nachos and beer, and there were games for the kids, who would buy stuffed horses and bulls. The rodeo was an evening of family fun.

He'd pay any price if he could give that to Renee.

He'd do anything to change the past. To do a better job of shielding her from an abusive, controlling mother and the scandals of her father. If he could go back, he'd give Clint a job, one that was legal and legit—one that would keep him out of jail.

"I need to leave," Renee said quietly.

"I'll go with you."

She made a huffing noise that might have been laughter or it might've been frustration. "No, you won't."

"But—"

"You don't get it, do you?" She pivoted in her seat and pinned him with a hard look. "I will ruin you, Oliver Lawrence. I'll ruin you and your business and everyone you love. And I won't do it. I…" Her voice cracked and she looked back out the windshield. "I can't do that to you."

His mouth opened but nothing came out.

"I need to pack," she said, her voice strong and sure again. "And then I need to leave before it all comes crashing down on you. I won't let my family destroy yours like they've destroyed me."

Thirteen

Oliver kept talking. One minute, he was going to charter a plane. The next, a helicopter. Then it was a private yacht leaving from Galveston and heading for open waters because "no one could follow us there," as if determined reporters wouldn't be able to rent a speedboat.

Renee listened with only half an ear as she packed because it didn't matter—whatever harebrained scheme he came up with, it wouldn't work. There was no quick, easy fix that would let everyone live happily-ever-after. Not this time. Not for her.

She knew that. She'd always known that. Funny how thinking it, however, made her heart ache.

She needed to leave quickly before Oliver got it into

her head to *make* her stay or, worse, enlist his family. Renee knew what she had to do but if the entire Lawrence family showed up to plead their case, she might not be strong enough to do the right thing.

And the right thing was so obvious. Renee simply couldn't hurt any of the Lawrences. Not even Flash. After all, he hadn't done anything Oliver himself hadn't done. Oliver had just had the good fortune to blurt out her name in front of small-town firefighters instead of a desperate music promoter.

So her mind was made up. She was leaving—alone. She'd see if she could stay with her former sister-in-law, Carolyn, for a few days. It would be awkward and uncomfortable but then again, Carolyn had given that interview where she'd passed on the chance to destroy Renee. And she and Carolyn had always got along before the scandal and divorce and death.

Besides, it wasn't like she could do more damage to Carolyn's reputation. She'd already been married to Clint. In the ruined department, she and Renee were practically equal.

Renee and Oliver would never be equal. Good Lord, he'd proposed. He'd said he'd marry her in the middle of the rodeo and he hated the rodeo.

In another time, another life, it would've been something wonderful.

Except for the *but*. Because there was always a *but*, wasn't there? As sweet as that marriage proposal had been, Oliver had prefaced that declaration with, *If I thought it'd make things better...*

He'd marry her. He'd do his best to make her happy. He might even adopt her child, when the time came, and she knew he'd be an amazing father. It might be good. Great, even.

But it wouldn't be perfect because he couldn't live without her. He'd offer her the protection of his name and access to all his resources because it was the most obvious solution to a problem.

Her.

She might be hopelessly in love with him, but she wasn't his problem to solve. And she wasn't about to marry another man who didn't love her.

Leaving was the only option.

"...one of those big bus-sized RVs that rock stars travel in," he was saying when he growled and spun, pulling out his phone. He never kept the sound on and therefore, she was always startled when he'd answer it at random times. "What?"

She hadn't bothered to pack the funereal dress or shoes—neither fitted anymore. But her lawyers would most likely blow their collective tops if she were spotted walking around in Chloe's fancy rodeo clothes. But the only alternative was pushing her leggings past the point of decency, so sequins it was. Which left the problem of the boots. She couldn't exactly walk around in those things anywhere but Texas. If she showed up in New York in the boots and the sequins, the press would have a freaking field day with her. What a shame. She set them next to the closet door and then closed the zipper on her single piece of luggage.

"Renee?" There was something different in Oliver's tone instead of the desperation that had colored all his grand plans thus far.

"Yes?"

"There are some men here for you."

The way he said it made it clear that he wasn't talking about the press. Even as the bottom of her stomach fell out, she squared her shoulders and lifted her chin. Old habits never died, it seemed. Just because she hadn't had to fall back on them for the better part of a month didn't mean she'd forgotten how to protect herself. "Who?"

But she already knew because Oliver wasn't trying to arrange a quick getaway in his zippy sports car. "The FBI. Security checked them out. They need you to return to New York with them."

Ah. They must have decided to turn the pressure up on Clint. At least, she hoped that was the case and not that they'd already caught wind of the disastrous rodeo outing.

Again, her stomach tried to turn at the thought of someone snapping a picture of her smiling and laughing—the very things her lawyers had informed her not to do. But Oliver had reminded her how to be happy and she'd almost forgotten what it was like to keep her real self locked deep inside.

She needed to remember. Quickly.

"I see." She tried to smile for Oliver, to show him that she wasn't scared or worried—that she'd be perfectly safe in the company of the Justice Department's best officers.

She didn't make it. "Don't do that," he snapped, throwing his phone down and closing the distance between them. He grabbed her by the shoulders. "Don't act like everything is fine when it's not."

She was leaving. Things might never be fine again. "You can't fix this, Oliver."

"The hell I can't," he said and slammed his mouth down over hers.

He meant it as a kiss of possession. Renee knew that. He wasn't going to let her go without a fight, fool that he was. But Renee knew the truth.

This was goodbye.

She wasn't going to cry.

Once upon a time, the Lawrence family had shown her what love was. They'd given her another life, one where people were sweet and loud and messy and loved. So, *so* loved. If she hadn't had that second childhood with Chloe, she didn't know how she'd have survived.

Oliver might not ever realize it because, knowing him, he'd look back at this moment and see nothing but a failure to fix everything just so. But he'd given her the same gift again. Love and happiness and a glimpse into a future she might one day have. He'd let her find her own way and made her laugh again.

She'd be forever grateful for this month.

But she couldn't tell him any of that without breaking down into sobs and she knew damned well that if she so much as wavered, he'd do something stupid like bust out the high-powered attorneys and call a press conference and all but announce to the world that he'd been sleeping with the pregnant Preston Pyramid Princess, and that?

That would be his downfall.

So, when the kiss ended, she pressed her lips against his cheek and gave him one final hug. "Goodbye, Oliver." Then she grabbed her solitary piece of luggage and hurried for the door before she changed her mind.

"Damn it, Renee, I can fix this! I just need more time," he said, sounding half-mad with desperation. "By the time the FBI is done with whatever they need you for, I'll have this figured out—I promise."

No, she couldn't be his problem.

So she kept walking.

She didn't look back.

Fourteen

Goodbye, Oliver.

Fuck that shit.

After nearly running over two photographers staked out by the garage entrance, Oliver stepped off the elevator. The door to his father's condo swung open seconds later, making it clear that Milt Lawrence had been waiting for him. Just when he thought the day couldn't get worse...

"Beer?" Milt said, holding up a longneck, and Oliver knew he didn't have much say in the matter.

He supposed this wasn't a surprise. Renee's brief appearance three days ago at the All-Around All-Stars Rodeo—brought to you by Lawrence Oil—in the company of Oliver Lawrence, head of Lawrence Energies, had made headlines less than an hour after Renee had been whisked back to New York in the company of the FBI's finest. The whole debacle was exactly the sort of thing that would draw Milt out of his hunting lodge and into the city.

Not for the first time, Oliver wished his father hadn't bought the condo next to his for those rare trips into Dallas. Being called in for a lecture had a way of making Oliver feel like he was twelve again and about to be grounded for another prank gone wrong.

Except this time, it wasn't an elevator and a bunch of balloons filled with shaving cream. This was the family business. Their livelihood. He'd risked an international energy company and his family's financial safety and well-being for...

For Renee. Who'd walked away without a look back.

God, it hurt.

It turned out that Brantley Gibbons, Brooke Bonner's manager, had lost a lot of money to the Preston Pyramid. In fact, he was under investigation because several of his clients claimed he'd inappropriately invested their funds with Preston's firm. Brooke had stuck by him because Gibbons was her uncle.

Family. Was there any bigger blessing and curse than that word?

"Here," Milt said, handing Oliver a beer and motioning for him to sit on the leather sofa overlooking the skyline. Unlike his hunting lodge, Milt Lawrence's condo was as impersonal as a hotel. Probably why he only spent maybe ten nights a year here. "Well, this is a fine how-do-you-do you've got yourself into."

Oliver gritted his teeth. "Do you think that, just once, we could cut the cowboy crap, Dad? Because I'm not in the mood to hear about how I look lower than a rattler's belly in a wheel rut." He took a long pull on his beer. It didn't help. "No offense." Oliver braced himself to be dressed down because with that attitude, he deserved it.

But that's not what happened. "I take it she'd been with you since you first asked if I'd heard about the scam?" To Oliver's ever-lasting surprise, there was less drawl in his father's voice. Still a little bit, though.

It was enough. "Yeah. A month." A good month. One of the best he could ever remember having.

Because Renee had been there. For the first time in years—maybe decades—Oliver had done something more than look at the family business or his family as just problems waiting to be solved.

He wasn't able to go back to who he'd been before Renee.

"Do you know where she is now?"

"New York." She wasn't responding to his texts, beyond the bare-bones information to let him know she was fine. Everything, apparently, was fine.

He was *not* fucking fine.

"She said she had to leave because she'd ruin me. I think she actually believes that," he said before taking another long swallow of his beer. It still wasn't helping.

"Hmm," Milt said noncommittally.

"She said…" He had to swallow a few times to make sure his throat was working right. "She said she wouldn't let her family ruin mine or my business like they ruined her."

"Ah," Milt unhelpfully added.

"That's it? That's all you've got? *Hmm* and *ah*?"

"I was going to say something about rattlers but that didn't seem to be the way to go."

"Jesus, Dad, are you mocking me?" There were days when his father was every bit as irritating as Flash—and worse.

"Simmer down, son." He held up his hands in surrender. "I'm not here to fight. If you're looking to take a swing at someone, either find your brother or go punch Clint Preston. Doubt either would help in the long run, though."

They sat for a moment. The silence was getting to Oliver, which had to be the only reason why he kept talking. Either that or the beer was actually starting to work and he just couldn't feel it. "I asked her to marry me and not only did she not say yes, she said goodbye." All that armor had been so locked in place that he still couldn't tell if she would've said yes or not had circumstances been different.

If the FBI hadn't shown up, would she still be here—or there or wherever he could have safely hidden her away? Or would she still have walked?

"Did she, now? In general, women like a nice proposal," Milt managed to say without laughing.

Oliver drank some more. Had it been, though? A nice proposal, that was. He'd said…

If he'd thought it would help.

Shit.

"She said she wasn't my problem to solve," he admitted, feeling suddenly stupid.

"Ah," Milt said again.

Oliver didn't dignify that with a response.

But had he actually said those words to Renee? He'd been upset, yeah. Flash had blown Renee's cover and Oliver had been frantic with worry about the best way to keep her safe but…

It hadn't been a nice proposal. Hell, it'd barely qualified as such.

"Do you know," Milt began, and for the first time in years, Oliver heard New York in his father's voice, "what I would give to have another day with your mother?"

Oliver let that thought roll around his head as he finished his beer and got up to get another. "Everything," he said when he settled back on the couch next to his father. "You'd give everything to have her back."

"You're damn right I would. The company, the rodeo, the lodge…" Milt cleared his throat and Oliver made sure not to look because he didn't want to see his father wiping away tears. "*Anything* to have her back."

"I'm sorry it's not going to happen," Oliver said. His mother's death was a problem he'd never be able to fix.

"And you know why I'd give everything for her?"

Oliver did look at his dad then. "Because you love her." There was no past tense about it.

"You're damn right I do." He stood, knocking back the last of his beer. "Herb Ritter's in town and I've got to smooth his ruffled feathers. And don't think I don't know you gave Chloe those negotiations after I told you not to. But Oliver?"

Oliver unclenched his teeth. "What?"

His father stared down at him with love and worry in his eyes. "We aren't your problem, either." He put a hand on Oliver's shoulder. "I know what you promised your mother, and she'd be right proud of you and everything you've accomplished. But we can take care of ourselves." He sighed. "We always could."

Then he grabbed his hat and walked out of the condo, leaving Oliver alone with his thoughts.

He couldn't function without Renee. He loved watching her try a new recipe and sharing in her success. Hell, he loved her failures, too—because they were always hilarious and only occasionally a hazard to home and health. He loved watching her grow and change with her pregnancy and he absolutely hated that she wasn't next door, waiting to welcome him home with a kiss that became so much more.

Holy hell, he loved her. Scandal-ridden family, broke, pregnant with another man's child—he loved Renee exactly as she was.

He hadn't told her that. Instead of treating her like the woman he wanted to spend the rest of his life with…

he'd treated her like a problem that he was responsible for solving.

Jesus, what had he done?

Because now she was thousands of miles away, facing lawyers and officers and, worse, her family without anyone to back her up while he sat here and got scolded by his father.

What the hell was wrong with him? She wasn't the problem. *He* was.

He loved her.

That was worth risking everything.

"And have you had any other contact with anyone in your family?" the bored federal prosecutor asked.

Frankly, Renee was bored, too. She'd been sitting in this conference room for the last three hours, answering the same questions she'd answered a few days ago with the same answers, which were the same questions she'd answered a few months ago. She was pretty sure the prosecutor was wearing the same suit.

"The friend I stayed with in Texas spoke with Clint, but only to confirm that I had nothing to do with the scheme."

That got the prosecutor's attention. "He did?"

"Oliver Lawrence was a childhood friend. He runs Lawrence Energies. He wanted to make sure I was being honest." Renee cleared her throat. It hurt to think of Oliver right now. "Trust but verify, right?" The prosecutor didn't so much as blink and Renee felt that old fear of having done something wrong roil her stomach. "I did get permission to go."

The prosecutor conferred with his secretary, who made notes as the prosecutor said, "Anything else?"

Renee unlocked her phone and called up the most recent text message from her mother. "I got this two days ago." She handed the phone over because there was no way in hell she was going to read that message out loud.

Someone had got a shot of her at the rodeo. Renee had actually thought it wasn't as bad as some of the paparazzi shots and she liked the way Chloe's jeans had looked on her. But her mother had, of course, felt it necessary to remind Renee how fat and embarrassing she was—especially in those clothes. Sequins were against her mother's rules, to say nothing of actual blue jeans. The horrors.

Renee hadn't even finished reading it. She was a grown woman, an expectant mother. She did not have to let her mother into her life anymore. Her parents had never loved her—or Clint. She owed them nothing.

The secretary made more notes and Renee forwarded a screenshot to the lawyer's email. "What else do you need from me?" Because no one had escorted her to Rikers or arranged for transportation. She was here to plead with Clint, wasn't she?

The bored prosecutor looked over his notes again and Renee fought the urge to roll her eyes. Finally, the man said, "Ms. Preston-Willoughby, Clinton Preston has accepted a plea deal in which he'll get a reduced sentence in exchange for testifying against Darin Preston."

"Oh." The word rushed out of her. "That's good. If I may ask…how reduced?"

"He'll plead guilty in exchange for a sentence of twelve years at a minimum-security prison with the possibility of parole. He might be out in seven." The prosecutor looked up at her. "I don't plan on letting your father out of prison in his lifetime, even if he pleads guilty to avoid a trial."

"Good." If the man was surprised by this, he didn't show it. "Will you be able to extradite my mother?"

That got her a faint smile. "If we do, will you be willing to testify against her?"

Renee thought about all those terrifying family dinners with forks repeatedly stabbed into her legs and being blamed for getting blood on her ruined pants and skirts. She thought about a lifetime of manipulation and deceit, of being made to feel small and hopeless and embarrassing.

Then she imagined her mother in the defendant's table, being forced to listen to Renee poke holes in her story of innocence one precise jab at a time. She smiled. Let her mother find out what real anxiety was like. "I'd be delighted to."

"I believe we have everything we need," the prosecutor went on. "If your father's case goes to trial, we'll expect your full cooperation." Renee nodded. That was always the deal. "Please don't leave the country and keep my office informed of where you are. Otherwise, you are free to go." He gave her that faint smile again. "Good luck, Ms. Preston-Willoughby."

She sat there for a moment, stunned. "I can go back to Texas if I want?"

Not that it was a good idea—it wasn't. She'd walked away from Oliver, after all. And he had paparazzi watching him now. She'd seen the pictures of him entering and leaving his building and Lawrence Energies's office complex. In every single shot, he was scowling. In all probability, she was probably lucky he hadn't punched anyone. But at least he wasn't running. He'd remembered that.

She'd done that. She'd taken away his privacy, not to mention Chloe and Flash's privacy. The Lawrence family was in the press in a highly public way.

"Of course. Get a job, move on with your life. We won't be garnishing your wages or any wages of anyone you marry."

Renee's mouth almost, *almost* dropped open at that, but those old damned habits kept her face blank. The prosecutor was just as unreadable but she shouldn't have been surprised. The man was no idiot.

"That's good to know. Thank you."

She and her lawyers stood, as did the prosecutor. Everyone shook hands. "Good luck," the man said.

She almost laughed at that. She'd been born to privilege and she was lucky enough to have known the love of the Lawrence family. But beyond that?

She'd been lucky enough to have a good month with Oliver. To ask for more than that would be too much.

She said goodbye to her lawyers and then hurried to the ladies' room. Her bladder seemed smaller every day. Her baby was growing. She could focus on impending motherhood now. That would be enough.

Lost in thought about what kind of job she might be able to get—something anonymous would be great—she exited the elevators into the lobby and headed for the door. She could see the paparazzi milling around outside but she didn't care anymore.

"I thought you hated the paparazzi."

That voice. *His* voice. "Oliver?" Renee stumbled as she whipped around, searching for him. Please, *please* don't let her be imagining his voice.

"But here you are, about to walk right out into their waiting cameras." He guided her to the side so effortlessly that she wasn't sure her feet touched the ground.

"You're here," she whispered as he pulled her into a waiting elevator. His arm went around her waist and he pulled her against his chest. God, she'd missed him. The five days since she'd forced herself to walk away from him had been a new, different kind of misery. She threw her arms around his neck and held on tight as the elevator doors slid shut. "What are you doing here?"

"Looking for you." He hit the button for the garage level and they began to move. "I made you a promise."

"You did?" She searched her memories and her heart sank.

He'd promised Clint he'd look after her.

Oh, no. He wasn't here because he couldn't live without her. He was here because he had a promise to keep. This wasn't any different than him offering to marry her because it might help. Oliver Lawrence was the most honorable man she'd ever known. Even though she'd walked away from him, he was going to take care of her. Whether she wanted him to or not, apparently.

"You don't have to do this," she said, her voice too soft. She was too soft when it came to him. Because she'd walked away once with her head up and her shoulders back. She wasn't sure she could do it again.

"I do." He lifted her chin so she looked him in the eye. "I promised I wouldn't leave you without saying goodbye."

She reared back, but he didn't let her go. He *had* promised that, hadn't he?

"But…" she said, staring at him. "I said goodbye."

"I didn't." Her breath caught in her throat at the sound of his voice, deep and intense. Oliver's eyes darkened. "What do you want, Renee?"

Before she could come up with an answer, the elevator dinged again and people got on. Oliver shifted so that Renee was standing next to him but his arm stayed locked around her waist and, fool that she was, she leaned into him.

He was really here. He was warm and he smelled like Oliver and he was wearing cowboy boots in New

York with his suit, and if she wasn't careful, she was going to burst into tears.

Her brother had agreed to a plea deal. Her father was never getting out of jail and, with any luck, her mother would be locked up before too much longer.

Renee was free to do whatever she wanted.

So what did she want?

They rode in silence the rest of the way down to the parking garage. He led her to a chauffeured car. The driver hurried to open the back door for her and Oliver guided her inside.

It was only when the door was shut that Renee found her voice. "What…"

"You didn't really think I was going to let you walk into that crowd of sharks and try to hail a cab, did you?" He shook his head like he'd told a joke.

"Oliver," she said, aiming for a sharper tone. His eyes softened as he folded her hand in his. "What are you doing here?"

"Coming for you."

She blinked and then, when nothing changed—he was still staring down at her with those warm brown eyes, still looking at her like he was glad to see her.

How was any of this possible? She'd seen the headlines. The wild—and not always wrong—guesses about the nature of her relationship with Oliver. The firefighters telling how she'd almost burned down the ranch house. Hell, someone had even got Lucille to give a comment. True, it'd been "Private people are entitled to private lives. Now, get off my porch or I'll shoot," but still.

"You know if we're seen together again, it'll only make things worse for you."

Everything soft and happy about Oliver hardened in a heartbeat. "Renee, what do you want?"

Her eyes watered instantly and she had to turn to look out the darkened windows of the car. They were out of the garage now and slowly creeping past the paparazzi waiting for her outside the building. She wondered how long they'd wait. Hopefully hours.

"I don't want to cost you your business," she said because it was the truth.

He snorted. She jerked her head around to stare at him. "Renee. What do *you* want? In the next five minutes or the next five years. What you want. Not what you or anyone else thinks you should do."

Her throat got tight and somehow, a lifetime of training herself not to cry began to fail her now. Because Oliver was the only person who'd ever asked and actually listened to the answer. "I don't want to hurt you."

"Oh, babe." He moved, pulling her onto his lap. She curled into him. "You know what I want?"

She shook her head against his shoulder.

"I want to take long walks around the park and maybe trail rides on the ranch. I want to see first steps and hear first words. I want to come home to fresh-baked cookies and spend nights in bed with you and wake up in the morning knowing you'll be right there.

I want to be by your side, in sickness and in health, in scandal and in quiet times—hopefully more quiet than this," he added with a chuckle.

"But why?" She sniffed. "Why would you risk everything for me?"

He tilted her face up and stared into her eyes. "Because I love you."

Her breath caught. She wanted that life, too. She wanted to raise her baby with him and know that he'd always be there for her. He'd never leave her and never cheat on her because he couldn't live without her. Not because she was a promise he had to keep.

"I *love* you, Renee," he repeated again, putting more force on the words. He tilted her chin up so she had to look at him. "And you know what?"

"What?"

"You're worth more than any business or house or even swans. I'd give all of it up in a heartbeat, just as long as you were by my side. My father, my siblings—they're all grown adults. They can take care of themselves. I don't have to do anything for them. I only have to do what I want. And what I want is to marry you. I want to love you for the rest of our lives. That's all I want."

She gasped. As declarations went, that was pretty damned good. Much better than offering to marry her if it'd help. But there was still one giant, huge problem. "I can't be your problem to solve, Oliver. I can't. That's not a life."

She braced for him to start a running list of why he could protect her, how he could take care of her—just like he'd done when she'd been outed at the rodeo. But instead, he touched his forehead to hers. "I'm always going to do my best to make things easier for you. Not because you're my responsibility but because that's what you do for someone you love."

When she didn't say anything, he cupped her face and kissed her. "Tell me what you want. Forget the cameras and our families. Just you and me, babe. We're the only ones who matter."

"I want it all," she sobbed. Stupid hormones. "I want to bake and crochet and take care of my baby. I don't want nannies or chefs or… Well, Lucille is okay. But I just want us. I want to know that you won't lie to me and I won't lie to you. I want to know you'll come home at the end of the day and we'll spend the evening together as a family. I want to hang out with Chloe and be irritated by Flash. I want…" She was crying so hard she could barely talk. "I want to be a Lawrence. I've *always* wanted to be a Lawrence. I want a big, happy family where everyone is loud and messy and loved and no one hurts anyone. And I want that with you."

"Oh, babe." His voice sounded choked as he wrapped her up in a huge hug and let her cry. When she'd calmed down a little, he looked her in the eyes. His thumbs rubbed over her cheeks, erasing her tears. "Renee, I promise you—I will never lie to you or cheat on you. I will always be there for you and make sure you have the space you need to find your own path forward. I'm not going to give up on you and I'm not about to let a little notoriety drive me away. You know why?"

"Why?"

"Because you—both of you," he added, resting a hand against her belly, "will always be family. Because I love you."

"I love you, too. God, Oliver, I love you so much."

He kissed her again and again and she lost herself in his touch, his taste, his smell. God, he smelled so good. Renee had no idea how much time had passed before the car made a wide turn, startling her back to her senses. "Where are we going?"

Oliver gave her that smile that, had she been standing, would have weakened her knees. "We're going home."

Finally.

Home was with Oliver.

Epilogue

"Up next on ESPN, June Spotted Elk has an exclusive interview with the Princess of the All-Around All-Stars Rodeo, Chloe Lawrence, about how the All-Stars are about to break big."

Pete Wellington's head popped up from the report on cattle prices he was working on. Not that there were many cattle left—but even if there were, at these prices, he'd never be able to pay the mortgage off. "What the hell?"

He caught a glimpse of the one woman who could make his blood boil with nothing more than a smile. Because Chloe Lawrence was smiling at the screen and his blood hit boiling in 0.2 seconds.

The camera cut to June, the world-famous bull rider.

"Bull riding brings in the big money. How can the All-Stars compete with the Total Bull Challenge?"

Pete's eyelid began to twitch as the camera cut back to Chloe. She flipped her rich auburn hair over her shoulder, the rhinestones on her shirt—unbuttoned just far enough to hint at the tantalizing curves of her breasts—sparkling in the lights. But nothing outshone her smile. That damned woman simply glowed. "For starters, I'm hoping to get you to ride on our circuit!" The women laughed. "We'll be introducing more women competitors," Chloe went on.

God forgive him, she was nothing short of perfect, which only made his ridiculous attraction that much worse. How many people tossed and turned at night because she haunted their dreams with that smile, those lips, that body? How many woke up hard and aching for her?

Probably too many to count. Pete took comfort that he wasn't alone.

But no one else saw her for what she was. The rest of the world bought into her stupid cowgirl persona.

He didn't want her. Hell, his life would be that much better if he never heard the names Chloe or Lawrence ever again. Pete's body might crave hers, but his brain knew the truth.

Chloe Lawrence was no cowgirl. She was nothing but a thieving, cheating liar, from a long line of cheats and thieves. The Lawrence family were little more than con artists and criminals. They'd stolen Pete's rodeo, his family ranch—his entire life.

Now she was ruining his rodeo. The one her father maintained that Pete's father had lost fair and square in a poker game. But Pete knew better.

When it came to Chloe Lawrence and her damned family, Pete Wellington had one goal and it had nothing to do with the way he ached for her.

He wanted his life back. And he was going to start by getting *his* rodeo back.

Even if he had to steal it out from under her nose.

* * * * *

If you loved this family drama and sensual scandal,
pick up these other titles from Sarah M. Anderson!

A MAN OF HIS WORD
A MAN OF PRIVILEGE
A MAN OF DISTINCTION
PRIDE AND PREGNANCY
NOT THE BOSS'S BABY

Available now from Harlequin Desire!

* * *

If you're on Twitter,
tell us what you think of Harlequin Desire!
#harlequindesire

COMING NEXT MONTH FROM

HARLEQUIN® Desire

Available May 1, 2018

#2587 AN HONORABLE SEDUCTION
The Westmoreland Legacy • by Brenda Jackson
Navy SEAL David "Flipper" Holloway has one mission: get close to gorgeous store owner Swan Jamison and find out all he can. But flirtation leads to seduction and he's about to get caught between duty and the woman he vows to claim as his...

#2588 REUNITED...WITH BABY
Texas Cattleman's Club: The Impostor • by Sara Orwig
Wealthy tech tycoon Luke has come home and he'll do whatever it takes to revive his family's ranch. Even hire the woman he left behind, veterinarian and single mother Scarlett. He can't say yes to forever, but will one more night be enough?

#2589 THE TWIN BIRTHRIGHT
Alaskan Oil Barons • by Catherine Mann
When reclusive inventor Royce Miller is reunited with his ex-fiancée and her twin babies in a snowstorm, he vows to protect them at all costs—even if the explosive chemistry that drove them apart is stronger than ever!

#2590 THE ILLEGITIMATE BILLIONAIRE
Billionaires and Babies • by Barbara Dunlop
Black sheep Deacon Holt, illegitimate son of a billionaire, must marry the gold-digging widow of his half brother if he wants his family's recognition. Actually desiring the beautiful single mother isn't part of the plan, especially when she has shocking relevations of her own...

#2591 WRONG BROTHER, RIGHT MAN
Switching Places • by Kat Cantrell
To inherit his fortune, flirtatious Valentino LeBlanc must swap roles with his too-serious brother. He'll prove he's just as good as, if not better than, his brother. But when he hires his brother's ex to advise him, things won't stay professional for long...

#2592 ONE NIGHT TO FOREVER
The Ballantyne Billionaires • by Joss Wood
When Lachlyn is outed as a long-lost Ballantyne heiress, wealthy security expert Reame vows to protect her. She's his best friend's sister, an innocent... Surely he can keep his hands to himself. But all it takes is one night to ignite a passion that could burn them both...

Get 2 Free Books,
Plus 2 Free Gifts—
just for trying the Reader Service!

HARLEQUIN *Desire*

EXPECTING A LONE STAR HEIR
SARA ORWIG

TWINS FOR THE BILLIONAIRE
SARAH M. ANDERSON

YES! Please send me 2 FREE Harlequin® Desire novels and my 2 FREE gifts (gifts are worth about $10 retail). After receiving them, if I don't wish to receive any more books, I can return the shipping statement marked "cancel." If I don't cancel, I will receive 6 brand-new novels every month and be billed just $4.55 per book in the U.S. or $5.24 per book in Canada. That's a savings of at least 13% off the cover price! It's quite a bargain! Shipping and handling is just 50¢ per book in the U.S. and 75¢ per book in Canada*. I understand that accepting the 2 free books and gifts places me under no obligation to buy anything. I can always return a shipment and cancel at any time. The free books and gifts are mine to keep no matter what I decide.

225/326 HDN GMWG

Name	(PLEASE PRINT)	

Address		Apt. #

City	State/Prov.	Zip/Postal Code

Signature (if under 18, a parent or guardian must sign)

Mail to the **Reader Service:**
IN U.S.A.: P.O. Box 1341, Buffalo, NY 14240-8531
IN CANADA: P.O. Box 603, Fort Erie, Ontario L2A 5X3

Want to try two free books from another line?
Call 1-800-873-8635 or visit www.ReaderService.com.

*Terms and prices subject to change without notice. Prices do not include applicable taxes. Sales tax applicable in N.Y. Canadian residents will be charged applicable taxes. Offer not valid in Quebec. This offer is limited to one order per household. Books received may not be as shown. Not valid for current subscribers to Harlequin Desire books. All orders subject to approval. Credit or debit balances in a customer's account(s) may be offset by any other outstanding balance owed by or to the customer. Please allow 4 to 6 weeks for delivery. Offer available while quantities last.

Your Privacy—The Reader Service is committed to protecting your privacy. Our Privacy Policy is available online at www.ReaderService.com or upon request from the Reader Service.

We make a portion of our mailing list available to reputable third parties that offer products we believe may interest you. If you prefer that we not exchange your name with third parties, or if you wish to clarify or modify your communication preferences, please visit us at www.ReaderService.com/consumerschoice or write to us at Reader Service Preference Service, P.O. Box 9062, Buffalo, NY 14240-9062. Include your complete name and address.

HD17R3

SPECIAL EXCERPT FROM

H HARLEQUIN®

Desire

*When Lachlyn is outed as a long-lost Ballantyne heiress,
wealthy security expert Reame vows to protect her. She's
his best friend's sister, an innocent… Surely he can
keep his hands to himself. But all it takes is one night to
ignite a passion that could burn them both…*

*Read on for a sneak peek of
ONE NIGHT TO FOREVER by Joss Wood,
part of her **BALLANTYNE BILLIONAIRES** series!*

That damn buzz passed from him to her and ignited the
flames low in her belly.

"When I get back to the office, you will officially
become a client," Reame said in a husky voice. "But
you're not my client…yet."

His words made no sense, but she did notice that he
was looking at her like he wanted to kiss her.

Reame gripped her hips. She felt his heat and…
Wow…

God and heaven.

Teeth scraped and lips soothed, tongues swirled and
whirled, and heat, lazy heat, spread through her limbs
and slid into her veins. Reame was kissing her, and time
and space shifted.

It felt natural for her legs to wind around his waist, to
lock her arms around his neck and take what she'd been
fantasizing about. Kissing Reame was better than she'd
imagined—she was finally experiencing all those fuzzy
feels romance books described.

It felt perfect. It felt right.

Reame jerked his mouth off hers and their eyes connected, his intense, blazing with hot green fire.

She wanted him… She never wanted anybody. And never this much.

"Holy crap—"

Reame stiffened in her arms and Lachlyn looked over his shoulder to the now-open door to where her brother stood, half in and half out of the room. Lachlyn slid down Reame's hard body. She pushed her bangs off her forehead and released a deep breath, grateful that Reame shielded her from Linc.

Lachlyn touched her swollen lips and glanced down at her chest, where her hard nipples pushed against the fabric of her lacy bra and thin T-shirt. She couldn't possibly look more turned-on if she tried.

Lachlyn couldn't look at her brother, but he sounded thoroughly amused. "Want me to go away and come back in fifteen?"

Reame looked at her and, along with desire, she thought she saw regret in his eyes. He slowly shook his head. "No, we're done."

Lachlyn met his eyes and nodded her agreement.

Yes, they were done. They had to be.

Don't miss
ONE NIGHT TO FOREVER by Joss Wood,
part of her **BALLANTYNE BILLIONAIRES** *series!*

Available May 2018 wherever
Harlequin® Desire books and ebooks are sold.

www.Harlequin.com